THE PROBLEM WIT

THE PROBLEM WITH *love* POTIONS

A ROMANTIC COMEDY

KATIE BACHAND

Copyright @ 2021 by Katie Bachand
All rights reserved.

Copyright ensures free speech and the creativity behind it is preserved.

ISBN: 9798486206375

FIRST EDITION

Cover Illustration and Design by:
Owned by Katie Bachand, Author

Author Image by: Studio Twelve:52

The Problem with Love Potions is a fiction novel. Names, characters, places, incidents and plot lines are used fictitiously and are a result of the author's imagination. Thus meaning, any resemblance to persons alive or deceased, buildings, establishments, locals, or events is coincidental.

For Mark.

You make my life magical.

BOOKS BY KATIE BACHAND

SERIES

Taking Chances Series:
Becoming Us (Prequel)
Conflict of Interest (#1)
In the Business of Love (#2)
A Business Affair (#3)
Betting on Us (#4)

STANDALONES

Romantic Comedy:
The Problem with Love Potions

Christmas Novels:
Postmark Christmas
Waiting on Christmas
A Borrowed Christmas Love Story
The Worst Christmas Wife

JOIN KATIE'S NEWSLETTER!

Head to Katie's website at
www.katiebachandauthor.com
and join her newsletter for fun content, great deals, free books, and more.

Or, simply scan the QR code below.

Enjoy!

THE PROBLEM WITH LOVE POTIONS

CHAPTER 1

Alice smiled at poor Blanche. It must be hard to be seventy and still want to date all of the available men at the small-town watering hole. If Alice thought her pool of men was shrinking, the devil only knows what Blanche thought of her own.

But then again, she and everybody else at Witches' Brew, Alice's quaint coffee shop in downtown Lantern Lane, knew precisely what Blanche thought.

"I gave Tom that latte, and he didn't so much as bat an eye at me." Blanche pointed her finger at the board behind Alice that listed all of the *potential* benefits of her beverages. "It says right there it's supposed to enhance one's attraction to another. Now I don't know much about all that scientific mumbo-jumbo, but I think that ingredient there, the one that says *Dehydroepiandrosterone*," Blanche fumbled through the long, jumbled word, "right next to *testosterone*. I'm pretty sure that means sex!"

Alice didn't have to move her eyes around the room to hear the townspeople's thoughts. She didn't even have to be a witch to guess. But she was a witch, and she could hear their thoughts, so it took an impressive amount of willpower to hold a straight face and address Blanche's concerns.

Alice swiped a stray, fiery red curl off of her forehead and sent a silent little truth spell in Blanche's direction. Nobody noticed the spark that flicked Blanche in the nose or the way she stood a little straighter when the magic took hold.

"Blanche, I am so sorry you feel the *Love and Spice Latte* didn't have the desired effect. But, I wonder, can you tell me that you are absolutely certain that Tom drank the latte you gave him?"

Blanche stared at the ceiling like the previous day's memory was stored in a Rolodex hovering above her.

"You know," Blanche started, "I didn't *see* him drink it. I set it on his desk after I snuck into his office. I didn't want to get caught because that security guard at the front desk of that tiny clinic is a stickler for only letting people in that have an appointment or an illness."

Alice nodded and furrowed her brows, showing Blanche she completely understood and sympathized with her crazy antics. "Yes, I see. I believe you know Kane is the security guard there," Alice agreed, to keep Blanche talking, but couldn't resist bringing up the fact that everybody knew everybody in their little port town.

"Well, yes. Of course, I know Kane. But it's not like that does me any good. He doesn't give an inch. I try to schmooze my way in, but he's a stickler, I tell you. Anyway, after careful observation," Blanche lowered her tone and leaned in, "I learned that it takes him about 44 seconds to use the restroom. So, naturally, I realized that was my window of opportunity. I had to get in and get out. You know?"

Curious, Alice wondered aloud, "Blanche, did you happen to notice anybody paying unusual attention to you yesterday? Say – oh, I don't know – lingering around you, or hugging you, or complimenting you, or just, well, anything?" Alice bent over the counter and used one arm to hold her head on her fist and the other to casually gesture as she asked the question.

"You know, now that you mention it, Candice did race out of the clinic after me yesterday. Didn't even bother to change out of that god-awful clinic gown they give you. Looks like old sheets. And that terrible way it flaps open in the back – leaves *nothing* to the imagination. Anyway, she just raved over my cooking, and between you and me, I'm not that great of a cook. Then she gave me an unusually long hug before Tom came out and got her. I think she might have sniffed me once or twice, too. Strangest thing. But that really isn't the point here."

Alice heard Blanche speaking, but the air in the room had changed. A fog settled in as if her coffee shop became an open field on a cold, hazy morning. Everybody blurred in the gray. She wondered if the others could see it. But as she looked around the room, they were all going on about their day as if nothing was out of the ordinary.

Alice felt her heart thud against her chest, and when she saw him, it stopped her heart for a split second. Then he disappeared.

"What in the?"

"Alice, are you even listening to me?" Blanche reprimanded Alice for her blank, disinterested look.

Alice blinked twice, and suddenly the room was alive and bustling as it was before she had her vision.

Alice didn't get visions often, but when she did, they meant trouble. Just ask any player on their '03 high school football team. She'd envisioned the star quarterback going down with an injury and the team losing a heartbreaker. Of course, they didn't know she was a witch, but Riley, her cousin and best friend - and sports enthusiast - did. And Riley didn't talk to her for a week after it came true.

"Blanche," Alice started, wondering if she could dig any information out of one of the prominent members of the town rumor-mill, "have you heard anything about a new–"

"Alice! This is serious. I will not be distracted by questions about that new deputy, Sheriff Lane Paxon hired. Can you help me with your faulty drink or not?"

New deputy.

Law enforcement officers were typically an area where witches tended to tread lightly. But at least she got a bit of information.

Alice smiled sweetly. She supposed she could focus on the comical task at hand. Because, poor Blanche, she just needed somebody to love.

"Okay, Blanche," Alice began her instruction as she moved to the right to start making the *Love and Spice Latte,* "this is what I'm going to need you to do: take this latte, go straight up to Tom when he gets off work. Tell him you'd like to share a coffee with him if he has the time. Then walk with him down to the shore, and enjoy the sunset while you sip your drinks. By the time the sun goes down, I can almost guarantee Tom will be smitten."

Blanche looked more than satisfied. Especially when two lattes were handed over, and she learned they were both free of charge. Blanche darted for the door, yelling her *thanks* over her shoulder.

Alice watched Blanche leave and shook her head. Alice knew Blanche was headed straight to the clinic to wait for Tom.

"What'd you put in it?"

Alice turned to see Paige Haskell, her young, quirky, but undeniably beautiful employee, wrapping an apron around her waist to start her shift and grinned.

Paige suspected there was something magical in the beverages they sold, but she had never been able to prove it. And the countless times she asked Alice if she was a witch – as ridiculous as the question sounded – Paige could never tell if Alice was joking or not when she'd reply, *Of course, aren't we all?*

But Paige had made up her own mind. You couldn't be as striking as Alice, have her track record of broken hearts left in her wake, and an insane number of satisfied customers. Her drinks were delicious, but at the end of the day, a good coffee was just a good coffee. There had to be some kind of sorcery or magic at play.

Alice waited for Paige's thoughts to slow. "Nothing out of the ordinary. Just the usual cloves, ginger, nutmeg…times two. Poor Tom isn't going to know what hit him."

Paige rested against the counter and put her hands on her hips. "More like Blanche isn't going to know what hit *her* once Tom kicks in."

Alice touched a finger to the side of her nose and agreed, thinking *you have no idea.*

When the bell on the door chimed, the two women shared a laugh before Alice turned to greet the customer. When she turned, she froze, and all she could say was, "It's you."

THE PROBLEM WITH LOVE POTIONS

CHAPTER 2

Theo Parker was none-the-wiser, but he pulled into Lantern Lane when a stranger named Blanche was talking her way into two free lattes.

As he drove through the dense, tree-laden lane, Theo wondered why on earth the road he drove in on was still gravel. But he had to admit, the bumpy ride and the hazy layer of fog that accompanied it seemed more like an appropriate welcoming party than a nuisance.

He reminded himself he wasn't running. It was just a new experience. A minor, temporary relocation.

Was it his fault his buddy just happened to have an opening at their local Sheriff's Office? *No.* Was it a blow to his ego to transition from patrolling a massive city to a town of about one thousand? *Not at all.* Was he still a little bitter about the way his ex-girlfriend had left him for not one but *two* friends they'd shared since college? *Well, possibly.* But if anybody asked him, he'd deny it until his face matched his old blue uniform.

"What the–"

Theo's old truck rumbled over what his GPS showed as the final bridge into Lantern Lane. The change in the air was so sudden he stopped his vehicle and stuck his head out of the squeaking crank window. He turned and saw the fog, still thick as mud, huddled over the bridge. Then he sat forward again and stared at so many fall-colored oranges, reds, and yellows he had to blink a couple times to make sure he wasn't dreaming. The stark contrast seemed like he just passed through a portal into another world.

That crisp golden hue that so often accompanied the fall sunlight made everything look mystical. His eyes traveled along the road lined with trees that were still sporting their water-colored leaves. They paused only a time or two to take in the occasional apple tree. Then they finally settled on the tiny port town at the bottom of the hill.

If Theo wasn't so dead-set on sulking and feeling sorry for himself, he would have forced himself to enjoy the view. It might have been a year since his ex left him, but that didn't make the sting any less.

As he pressed his foot against the gas pedal to start down the hill, Theo's eyes caught two leaping dogs as they chased after a young boy. They were darn-near frolicking through a pumpkin patch.

"Oh, come on! Can't a man just be crabby for two minutes?"

When the dogs caught the boy, they all rolled on the ground. The dogs lapping at the youthful face while the boy laughed hysterically.

Theo couldn't stop the smile. "Okay, fine," he said to himself, accepting the moment with a slight grin. "But *just* this one. You have brooding to do. And all this happy sappy stuff isn't going to send the right message to people. Especially the women."

Seeing as he'd written women off, he figured the best way to go about this next phase of his life was to do it completely alone.

Theo's red truck with its rounded, old-style bumpers and fenders chugged into town and stopped with a clank. He threw the shifter into park and let his eyes travel the length of the street.

All of the buildings sat side-by-side. Some were brick, some had white wooden paneling, and some sported a shaker-style exterior that reminded Theo of New England.

He climbed out of his truck and stretched his muscles from sitting through the three-hour drive. It wasn't long, but the distance was enough to give him some breathing room and his mind some wide-open space. Not to mention the size of the small town. With a single stretch of main street, a short winding road that led to the water's edge, and only a thousand people that populated it, he figured he'd be safe enough.

Looking around, Theo noticed a diner, a coffee shop, a few outfitters, a book store, and a grocery store at first glance.

It had just about everything a man could ever need when embarking on a new journey. He breathed one more bracing breath, then zeroed in on the coffee shop. *Witches' Brew.*

Clever.

Theo appreciated the name. And after his initial analysis of the town, it fit perfectly. These people sure had an affinity for fall, what with the decorations on every doorstep and window. He wasn't sure he'd ever seen more pumpkins, broomsticks, or hay bales in his entire life. And his mom had been one of those decorating nut-jobs when he was growing up.

Theo walked toward the glorious scent of coffee. In fact, it nearly pulled him there. Had ground espresso ever smelled so delicious?

The scent dragged him to the door. In a trance, he pulled it open and stepped inside.

The shop was quaint. It had mismatched tables and chairs that somehow all fit together. The walls were stained a deep brown, and the floor was a simple brick pattern that seemed rustic, not by design but by age.

As his eyes traveled to the front of the shop, he watched an old woman who was grinning ear to ear rush away from the counter. If he hadn't stepped out of the way, she very well could have barreled him over on her way out of the door.

Theo laughed a bit at the humor of the sight, then refocused as something was drawing his attention back to the counter.

Then he saw her.

A wild, red-haired beauty, laughing at her conversation with the other woman behind the bar. When she looked up, their eyes met. Theo noticed hers were piercing green, and just below them, her nose sloped into an alluring pointed end.

His heart hammered, while in his mind warning sirens were blaring and flashing as bright as the misery lights that flashed on the top of his old patrol unit.

Then she spoke, and his emergency flares shot in all directions.

"It's you."

Her voice cast a spell over him. If he didn't get out now, he thought he might never be able to leave.

Theo watched as she thought about making a motion to move forward. This was ridiculous. He didn't know who this woman was, but apparently, she knew him. Maybe Lane Paxton, his old friend, told her about his arrival. It was a small town, he supposed that was possible. But, no matter the reason, he didn't want to be known by her – or any other woman for that matter.

Especially one that *looked* like she did.

Catching himself – and the woman, given her abrupt halt – by surprise, Theo just shouted, "No! No. Nope. Not gonna do it."

Theo backpedaled while she and the rest of the coffee shop watched his outburst. He tripped as he made his way through the threshold of the building, then said, "No way," before stumbling once more and pushing the door closed with more force than he intended.

Nobody on the inside heard the final *No*. But they did see the shape of his mouth form the word from the other side of the door before he set his rigid body in a straight line and turned to walk away.

CHAPTER 3

"He's here!"

Alice walked through the door of her best friend Riley's book shop. She didn't bother using the handle to open and close the door; a flick of her wrist handled the job for her just fine.

"With a customer," Riley sang from the back of the store to let Alice know there was a non-magical human in their presence. "Be right with you!"

Their code was efficient. Alice quickly finished her twitch to ensure the door closed without anybody witnessing her magic. She knew people talked, but it was better if the witches of Lantern Lane to stay *mostly* a secret.

Riley's long black hair was tied in a braid that hung over her shoulder, and her boyfriend-style jeans hovered over her brown high-top boots as she ushered her customer out.

Alice noted the woman walked out with two of the latest best-selling novels and one book on the town's history and the witches that were known to occupy it. All fiction – of course.

When the customer was safely out the door and out of earshot, Riley turned and folded her arms over the rusty-red flannel shirt she was wearing and said, "I'm going to need you to be a little more specific when you say, *he.*"

Alice put her hands on her hips and squinted at her friend.

"I know you know who I'm talking about," Alice said, finally when Riley stood as smug and stubborn as an old tree.

But she only received a shrug in return. "I don't know," Riley said, looking up as if she was trying to find the answer. Then she grinned. "It could be the wizard you haphazardly dated last month, your estranged father, or, I suppose, it could even be Grumbles, your dog." Riley pulled her arms apart and started moving back toward the stacks of books by the register. "Who, by the way, is going on seventeen."

"I don't want to talk about it." Alice turned up her nose but flicked a loving eye in Grumbles' direction.

"People are going to start asking questions."

Alice shrugged. "He's an anomaly. And the most loyal man that I've had in my life. And he's not the point."

"Just saying. Turn him into a cat or something."

Alice sucked in a sharp breath, then whispered, hoping that wherever Grumbles was, he didn't hear what had just been said.

"I would *never.* What an insult to a beautiful life."

"You *are* a witch. Cats are kind of a thing."

"Not a chance. Now, stop." Alice whipped a hand from across the room and neatly organized the books into the shelves that Riley was about to put away human-style. "I *know* you either saw it or felt it. He's here."

Riley did know. She had both felt it *and* seen it. She'd felt the vibration from Alice's heart all the way through the thick, brick building walls that separated them. And from

Riley's bookshop location at the bottom of the hill, she'd seen the billow of fog begin to part as the old red truck made its way through their barrier.

"Well, the good news is he didn't get gobbled up on his way in." Riley smiled.

"I *knew* you felt it."

Riley wandered to the table she used as a check-out counter and leaned on it. "So, what happened? Did he confess his love? Propose on sight? I haven't felt a pull that strong in, well…" Riley thought about it. "Ever, really."

"Not exactly," Alice admitted as the scene replayed in her mind.

Riley's finger pointed to a chair and drew a line on the floor. The chair she pointed to before the movement obeyed and slid over to her so she could sit.

"He came in, stood for a second, we locked eyes. I tried to talk to him in my…you know." Alice pointed to her head to indicate she'd tried to speak to his mind. "That didn't work." Alice darted eyes at Riley, knowing she'd only get a long lecture about applying her craft in study as well as organically. "And don't tell the aunts!"

Riley crossed a finger over her heart. "Secret's safe with me." Then her mind added *But I'll be sure to use it against you at some point.*

"Very funny," Alice said at Riley's easy grin that came along with the telepathic message. "Anyway, he took one look at me, looked like a big-eyed jack-o'-lantern, then yelled *no* as he backpedaled and tripped out the door."

Riley nodded, digesting the information. "Right. So, it sounds like you have it in the bag then?"

"You're really not helping." Alice squinched her lips to one side as her mind raced.

"You could ask the–"

"No. Absolutely not," Alice cut Riley off. She didn't need powers to know what Riley was going to suggest. Riley was going to say that she could ask the aunts. And that she could do it on *Spritz and Spirits Saturday.* Which had started as a once-a-year ode to the witches they lost during the Trials, but over time became more about the spirits of the wine and vodka-sodas variety that they could consume as they honored the dead. "You know I don't get into honoring the dead.*"*

Riley gave Alice another sly smile. "No, you don't love the aunts - or the dead. But as I recall, you're extremely good at the *Spirits* part."

Alice narrowed her eyes at her best friend. "It was *one time.* And everybody was naked that night." Alice tried to remember the evening's events clearly, but all she could ever conjure up was the potion she'd made herself the day after to cure the hangover.

While Alice's thoughts moved away from the memory of a night she was more than okay forgetting, her mind drifted back to the man she knew she would never be able to forget.

Alice was drawn to him, and he must have been to her. Only, he wasn't as on board with the idea. Nevertheless, Alice knew she needed to know him. She had only seen his face twice, once in her mind and once when he came to her. Then, of course, he ran away. But that, for now, was beside the point.

Which brought up the *other* reason she had to talk to Riley.

Alice tapped her finger on the table as she tried to figure it out on her own, but nothing came. A little spark flared with each tap – the uncontrolled result of too much magic and too little practice.

"Out with it before you burn the place down." Riley wafted a hand in Alice's direction, causing a brush of cold to whoosh over the counter.

Alice said it quickly, "I couldn't read him. I couldn't see inside him at all. Not even something as simple as his heartbeat or body temperature."

Riley squeezed her lips together in a smile. "You need the–"

Alice shot a finger at Riley. "Don't even say it."

"The aunts." Riley ignored the order.

Alice dropped her body into a chair that wasn't there and let her head fall to the table in a huff.

"They really aren't *that* bad," Riley leaned on the table, resting her head on her hands, so her face was nose-to-nose with Alice's when she looked up.

"They *really are*, though." Little worry lines folded across Alice's forehead.

Riley rubbed their noses together, as they had when they were little. "They're not. I'll go with you."

"You always go."

"I know. I'm the favorite niece."

"That's not fair."

"I know." This time Riley's kind smile didn't make fun.

When the bell on the book shop door chimed, neither woman bothered to look up right away.

"Morning. Do you happen to have any self-help–"

It was the thickness in the air that made her turn, but the dreamy, seductive voice forced her to lose her concentration.

As quickly as he noticed she was in the shop, she forgot she was sitting on air. Alice pulled the spell from her mind, and her body went crashing to the floor.

"What the–?"

Riley lurched her body over the table to look over the edge. "Hey," Riley said, dangling her head to hover over Alice, who was flat on her back, "are you okay?"

"It's him," Alice whispered, not to keep the secret, but because the air had effectively been knocked from her body.

"Were you just…?" Theo held up his hands when both women craned their necks to look at him. "You know what? Never mind."

They watched him turn, mumbling to himself. "A guy tries to get away. And what? His punishment is running into the same irritating, beautiful woman *twice* in ten minutes? *Come on!*"

Alice and Riley stared at the rant as he made his way out of the door. Their heads moved slowly, reaching as he turned to walk along the sidewalk in front of the town's buildings until he was out of sight.

"I'm going to take a leap off of a broomstick and say that *that* was him?" Riley asked, earning a look from Alice.

Pulling herself up off the floor, Alice stared at Riley.

"What?" Riley asked.

"Did you see?"

"See what?"

"You could see inside him, couldn't you?" Alice felt the overwhelming need to know. If Riley could see inside him, why couldn't she?

"I'm not telling."

"You could!" Alice accused as if Riley could control why Alice's magic didn't seem to be working on him.

"You need to see the aunts."

"I need to find out who he is." It was as if Alice didn't hear a word Riley said.

Alice turned to walk toward the door, deciding if she couldn't be a witch about it, she'd do her digging the old-fashioned way – small-town gossip.

"I still think you need to–"

"I will!" Alice yelled as she marched out of the door, agreeing that she'd go with Riley to see the aunts for *Spritz and Spirits*.

Alice paused just outside and looked down at the festive fall decorations that Riley had put up that morning. She turned back to Riley, who was leaning against the counter, arms folded once more, grinning. "Cute," Alice said as her finger made an arch, pointing to the décor.

Then she marched back to her coffee shop. Alice needed to find a way to lure that man to her.

CHAPTER 4

Theo had made it to day two in town, but barely. After the run-in at the book shop, he'd found his apartment rental then lost a battle with himself that staying was a good idea.

But even with the war going on inside his head, he had to admit, Lantern Lane was nice. Even on the overcast autumn day.

Theo was reluctant to admit it, but he'd always liked the fall. And something about the small town, the abundance of trees, fields of pumpkins and orchards – not to mention the town's cobblestone streets, and old black oil lanterns for nighttime lighting – it all seemed…enchanting.

The coffee he'd scrounged up from an old machine he'd found in the furnished apartment wasn't great, but it was the best Theo could do since he was forcing himself to avoid the woman who haunted his dreams the entire night.

He didn't know who she was, but he hated that he wanted to.

Theo wasn't scheduled to report to work until the next day, but he could head over to the Sheriff's Office and see Lane, get acquainted with the staff – or rather, the only other staff member – and be grateful for the diversion. He could casually ask around about the woman at the coffee shop, and with any luck, he'd find out he should avoid her at all cost. At this point, he'd take whatever reinforcement it could get.

On his way to the office, Theo was greeted by everybody he passed. Two of the passersby actually greeted him by name and welcomed him to Lantern Lane.

It was charming, he supposed. Better than his previous gig in the city, where people tended to look away and avoid him. He knew it was the uniform, but still, beneath the blue, he was just another guy.

After walking a couple of blocks, Theo spotted his friend – and now boss – Sheriff Paxton, walking out of Witches' Brew with two lidded paper cups in hand, holding the door open for a couple who were headed in. The sight of his old schoolmate felt good. No other way around it. It would be a good gig for a little while.

Theo picked up his pace to catch up. He supposed it maybe looked a little funny, but he had to do what he had to do. So, as Theo approached the outside of the coffee shop, he shielded his head with his jacket. Once hidden, he sprinted his way across the sidewalk, like a flash darting from one side of the windows to the other. In his mind, he felt the stares from the customers inside and people on the street, but all he could think was: *Its self-preservation, people.*

When he made it to the other side, he stood tall again, dropped his jacket, and shrugged himself back into place. Theo nodded and smiled casually at two ladies who had witnessed his sprint and acted like nothing was out of the ordinary.

"Now, where am I?" Theo tried to get his bearings, but he had to admit, he didn't do as good of a job studying the area as he should have. Heck, he'd even accepted the position from Lane sight-unseen.

Instead of struggling, he pulled out his phone and plugged in the address Lane had emailed him a week earlier. His phone spun, thought for a minute, then calculated his route.

"Thirty seconds away?" Theo said, reading his phone aloud. He looked up, across the street, and back again. Then he saw it, right in front of him.

Lantern Lane Sheriff's Department.

Theo looked at his phone, then the office. Then he closed his eyes and breathed before turning his head to the left and staring at the building right next door: *Witches' Brew.*

"I have to be cursed," Theo muttered before dropping his head.

He shook his head once with it still hanging down, realizing he would have to actively try and avoid the *literal* woman of his dreams, but he was determined. Theo righted his head, tossed his phone in his jacket pocket, and walked into his new office.

"Lane Paxon," Theo said when he spotted Lane hovering over the attractive office assistants' desk.

Was every woman in this town gorgeous? Maybe it's a right of passage here?

"A sight for sore eyes. How the heck are ya, buddy?" Theo asked, pushing away his thoughts.

"Theo Parker, as I live and breathe. It's been a couple years too many, but I finally got you out here." Lane gave Theo the same crooked smile he had as a kid when they were running around bases and down football fields together. A smile that could welcome a perfect stranger into feeling like they were the most important person in town.

"Well, I got sick of you begging, so here I am." Theo walked into the arms of his long-time friend and gave him a hug that was ten years overdue.

"As cute as this is, I'd like to meet our new deputy." An accent he couldn't quite place drawled out of the woman he'd seen sitting at the front desk when he walked in. It was alluring and cute, all wrapped into one purr of a voice.

Lane gave a laugh and one more squeeze of Theo's shoulders before he dropped his arms and turned, so they were both facing the woman who was now standing on the other side of the desk.

"Theo, this is Rebecca Bassett. She's the smartest woman in town and makes sure we, and the rest of 'em, toe the line. I'm mostly here to do the grunt work." Lane and Rebecca exchanged a smile before she turned her attention to Theo and extended a hand.

"Beck," she said while they shook hands. "People call me Beck. Rebecca's a hard name to have around here. Bad memories and what-not."

Theo smiled, immediately warming to the petite blonde-haired woman. It was cut short and had a slight wave to it. It seemed natural, but how could it just *be* that way?

Just like the coffee woman, Theo thought.

The fiery-red mass of curls should have been unruly. Instead, they framed her freckled face perfectly.

When he felt his hand start to warm, Theo snapped out of his daydream and quickly pulled it away.

"Ah, it's nice to meet you, Beck. Happy to hear somebody's keeping this guy in line." Theo motioned in Lane's direction, who was happy to sit and watch the interaction.

"Can I get you anything? Perhaps a coffee?" Beck offered a casual smile. "You seem like you could use one. I can tell when people have coffee on the brain."

Theo tried to pay no attention, but he felt as if his new assistant had been reading his mind. He knew offering coffee was the polite thing to do, but why did it feel like it was more than that?

Stop. He told himself. Overreacting was a ridiculous thing to do. And, to be honest, he'd been craving a good coffee since yesterday, but he hadn't been able to scrounge up the courage to get one.

If Beck went and got him one, it would solve two of his problems: a coffee craving and avoiding *the woman.*

"That settles it," Beck said, responding to only Theo's smile. "I'll head over and get you a coffee. Alice – the owner – I'm sure she'd love to have you in. Would you like to join me?"

"No!" Theo coughed and cleared his throat, hoping he didn't sound ridiculous. Then he said again, with a little more calmness, "Ah, no, thanks. I'll stay back and catch up with Lane. And thanks – for the coffee."

The two men watched as Beck pulled her bag from a drawer in her desk, tossed it across her body, and skipped out the door.

Theo waited until Beck was out of sight, then he slouched his shoulders and turned an eye on Lane.

"You seem a little jumpy today." Lane tried to read Theo's facial expression.

All Theo offered was a cautious laugh.

"Okay, fine. You're a day early," Lane said, with a playful slap on Theo's arm.

"I came early to catch some sights, walk around town. Get acquainted."

"And you're not doing that right now because…?"

"I came here to avoid beautiful women," Theo admitted, nodding quickly to avoid further discussion about it. "Also, for the job. But mostly, to avoid women."

The boom of laughter burst out of Lane. It was followed by a couple of heaves, the kind of laughter that can only be had when you're trying to catch your breath.

"This," Lane started while nodding his head toward the door, "is the *wrong* place to be if you're trying to avoid beautiful women."

"That's very *not* reassuring. I thought maybe I'd just happened to run into all three right off the bat. I thought maybe all the rest of the women looked similar to my mom, or grandma, or my great aunt Sue."

"Wow." Lane leaned against the desk next to Theo, so they were both sitting side-by-side. "Trish really did a number on you. I thought for sure you two were in it for the long haul."

"I suppose there was something in the back of my mind that had me holding off on buying a ring. But man…Lance *and* Chuck? That was a low blow."

Lane lifted a questioning brow.

Theo bobbled his head in acknowledgment. "Yeah, I know," Theo said, accepting the gesture. "Lance was bad enough."

"He just always had that creepy vibe, ya know?" Lane squinted off into the distance as if he was picturing their strange college acquaintance.

"Totally creepy," Theo agreed.

Man. Theo thought, it felt good to just say it out loud to a friend that had no judgment on the matter, just an excellent escape plan.

The men sat for another minute as Theo recovered from his break-up story, and Lane shook his head a few more times at his old friends' reality.

"Well," Lane began, "let's head back to my office. Why don't you tell me which woman, in particular, you're trying to avoid?"

Theo accepted the order and rose to follow Lane through the Sheriff's building.

The structure, on the outside, blended in with the town's old-world aesthetic. But, inside, it was more like a well-kept Victorian home than a place you'd keep law-benders and criminals for the night.

He eyed the combination of wood and brick that made up the walls. A brilliant fireplace was ablaze with a crackling fire that smelled like chestnut, sandalwood, and a hint of cinnamon. And old creaking doors led the way in and out of the single office on the main floor and what Theo assumed were the bathrooms and the holding cells toward the back.

"I'll get to that." Theo had to get to something that had been on his mind ever since he rolled in first. "But first, why does it feel like fall in Lantern Lane is on steroids?"

Lane pushed the door to his office open and left it that way as they walked in to take a seat. "Because it is. Ever since I moved here – which was right out of the program – it's been like this. Every year I think I'm going to get used to it, and I never do. I can't explain it. It's almost like it comes with the culture. Like the season knows this is when the people of

Lantern Lane really shine. I don't think I'll ever be able to leave because of it."

He wanted to poke fun – it's what buddies did – but Theo couldn't find it in himself to judge his friend when he'd felt the same thing. So instead, he nodded and sat in the chair Lane motioned to as Lane took a seat in his own chair on the other side of the desk.

"Well?" Lane asked, folding his hands and resting them on the desk. A display of patience that told Theo he could wait all day.

"I suppose I should start by saying: I didn't plan on actively avoiding any one particular woman. It was more: I just didn't expect to see a woman who dang-near knocked me off of my feet." Theo thought back to the day he arrived. "Full disclosure, I actually tripped on my way out of the coffee shop."

"Ahhh." Lane issued the drawl at learning who it was that happened to be driving his friend crazy. "Alice Balfour. She's the owner of the coffee shop. Gorgeous, peppy, people-skills for days." Lane smirked. "That explains the not wanting to head over to get your own coffee. Anyway, I've only ever had to investigate her once."

"Come again?" Now Theo was interested.

Lane leaned back for the short story. "Yeah, it wasn't a big deal. A woman who came through town for the Fall Festival – that's next week, by the way – tried accusing Alice of her husband's infidelity while they were here."

"She thought Alice slept with her husband?"

Lane laughed and lifted a brow at the question. "No, no. She thought there was something in her husband's latte that forced him to hit on pretty much every woman at the festival."

Theo grinned at the idea. He didn't know why he thought it was so funny. Probably the unrealistic nature of the accusation.

"What did Alice say?" Theo didn't have trouble imagining the stunning woman who hadn't left his mind since the day before. Of course, he didn't like it, but he did find the story amusing.

"Just showed her ingredient list. All-natural. All her recipes are approved by the Food and Drug Administration. No safety concerns." Lane shrugged. "Seems the lady married a man who had an eye for other women. So, Alice?" Lane's change of subject was about as discreet as getting a giant pumpkin thrown at your face.

When Theo huffed, he turned at the sound of Beck walking back into the office with a single paper cup. Her grin was wide and amused at stepping into the name of her good friend on the lips of men.

"No coffee for you?" Theo asked Beck as she handed him the cup. He enjoyed that the conversation with Beck seemed easy and natural. It would make the transition to the new office, and hopefully new friends, a lot easier. He also enjoyed that though she was beautiful, he wasn't attracted to her at all.

"Nope. My boss brings me coffee every morning. Perks of the job." Beck winked at Lane before handing the cup to Theo, then patted him on the shoulder.

"Alice asked about you. She would love for you to come in and say *hi.*" Beck didn't bother sticking around. With the fireworks she'd felt from both Theo and Alice, it wouldn't take long for them to cross paths – *whether Theo wanted to or not*. On that thought, Beck went back to her desk to prepare for the day.

"Oh, right. Ah, I'll think about it," Theo mumbled the words to Beck's good-natured suggestion, knowing they were out too late for Beck to have heard them.

"I can't watch this anymore. We might as well go tour the town so I can give you the low-down. Seeing you like this is…pathetic."

"Yeah," Theo admitted. "I know. We should go."

Theo kept his cup in hand, finally taking a sip before slipping out of the door back into the crisp fall morning.

"Really?" Theo stopped, causing Lane to run into his back.

"What now?" Lane asked, not knowing whether to laugh or be concerned.

Lane turned slightly to give Beck a look that said, *What in the heck is with this guy?* Beck had to cover her laugh so Theo wouldn't see their amusement when Theo turned around.

"Even the drink is…*her*. That's weird, right? I taste espresso, sugary cream, cinnamon, and…is that apple?"

Theo took another sip, and the image of Alice appeared in his mind, hitting him again, taking another swing at his avoiding-women resolve.

As Theo swallowed, he felt the easy-going laughter of a woman he'd never met and saw Alice so clearly he felt like if he reached out, he would be able to touch her.

Theo took one more sip because, well, it was delicious. But then, the principle of the matter took over. If he was going to avoid women, and now it seemed *one woman,* in particular, he was going to be all in.

After the fantastic, scalding gulp, Theo handed the steaming white cup back to Lane and said, "I'm quitting cold turkey."

Lane shook his head and took a sip. It was *terrific*, but all-in-all, he didn't see what the big deal was. Lane watched a determined Theo take confident strides out of the door. He turned left and started down the sidewalk to make their rounds.

Lane didn't move, just yelled, "Car's the other way."

Theo turned, keeping his head down, and walked back across the front of the building, moving in the other direction.

CHAPTER 5

It might have been part of her *nature.* Or, she supposed, it could have been a time of the year when the moon started to play tricks on the sun. When the air grew a bit more mysterious, and the night crept in on the day. But, whatever the reason, fall was Alice's favorite time of the year – and her favorite time to conjure up new potions and spells. -

There had been a time when she and the other witches would have gathered in late summer to push out the warm weather. They'd cast a circle using brooms and bodies at Willa's family farm and enchant the town. They'd call for the earth and the wind to shift, and they'd call for the residents to embrace the motion. It created the perfect combination of nature and nurture. The season would change, and the people would cherish its offerings.

Over time, Alice and her family and friends would go out onto the field, only to realize the earth had already listened. So rather than change something that had already been perfected, they stayed to gather and enjoy an autumn dinner.

That was over two months ago now. Still, the golden hue showed no sign of leaving, and Alice loved it.

She hummed back and forth from her wardrobe to an oversized mirror that sat on the floor, resting against her bedroom wall. With her, she brought different outfit combinations she'd considered, then discarded.

Usually, at just past four-thirty in the morning, she'd be ready to take the back steps from her pint-sized condo above the coffee shop, into the back door of Witches' Brew, and start prepping for her day. But today, she wanted to look irresistible.

After a night of dreaming about Theo – she'd learned his name from Beck – Alice decided she needed to make a move. If the feelings she'd had so far were any indication of the man and all that was possible between them, she *needed* to know him. The pull was so strong she felt herself drift into his dreams. His stubborn mind tried to keep her out, but fortunately for her, the heart usually won out when it came to magic.

And, if she took matters into her own hands, she wouldn't have to go see the aunts.

Instead, she could casually show up at the places he would begin to frequent or pop up during random outings that he would take during the day or in the evening. It wasn't uncommon to run into somebody at the grocery store or the diner in this town.

Besides, if she found a way to get close to him, maybe she could figure out why her pull to him was so strong. And, it just might save her a lecture from the aunts and probably keep her from drinking too many bottles of wine the next time she was forced to stop by.

Finally settled on a rust-colored sweater and a flowy knee-length flannel skirt, Alice decided to twist her hair back into a long, full ponytail of curlicues. Then, with a tap of her finger on her cheeks, she turned them a rosy rouge color, and as she washed her hands, she updated her fingernails from the shiny black she'd worn the day before to a pretty burgundy to match her outfit.

Alice reached out for her purse that was sitting across the room and called down the hall while it floated over to her. "Grumbles! Time to go."

Grumbles meandered over to her, as only a dog who looked as big as a horse could, and nudged her hip. The big brown dog was the size of a mountain and as cuddly as a teddy bear.

"*Turn you into a cat,* she said." Alice bent down to nuzzle Grumbles' forehead and rub his ears that had perked up at the terrible idea. "Don't worry, Big Guy. I told her she was crazy. Ready to head down?"

The low *gruff* was his agreement, and he plopped down the steps to the Witches' Brew after Alice.

When they made it down the stairs, they saw the lights were on, and music was blaring.

Over the years, Alice had learned to enjoy the yearning and the agonizing hard tempo of Paige's alternative taste. There were worse things that she could be forced to listen to. And when the doors opened at five-thirty, the hard yelling would change to the light, cool melody of a coffee shop blend.

Grumbles started wagging his tail to the beat and trotted over to Paige, who was waiting for him with a pile of whipped cream. It took a lot for Grumbles to go anywhere except his plush bed that sat right next to the coffee bar, but he didn't disappoint. As soon as he lapped up every speck of white fluff from the cup Paige was holding out for him, he waited for his routine scratch on the head, then circled himself over the pillow before plopping down and falling into a deep, doggy sleep.

"You're extra cute today. Want to tell me why?" Paige pointed a finger at Alice before turning to finish powering up the giant vats of coffee that would make the room fill with the best smell in the world.

Was there anything better than the thick, roast-y scent of freshly brewed coffee?

Alice grinned. Was there really any use in hiding what she was doing? She remembered the dreamy way Theo had stumbled backward out her door. How adorable his mumbling was. How undeniably cute his fluster was.

"Oh my gosh, it's the guy, isn't it?" The excitement from Paige was evident in her voice and in the way she lurched at the stereo controls to turn the volume down so she could give her full attention to every detail.

Alice wanted to be giddy. But, even for a witch, the idea of a complete stranger consuming her every thought was a bit…well…strange. So, she tried to play it cool.

"I can't stop thinking about him!" The words shot out of her mouth as she rushed over to lean on the same counter as Paige.

So much for playing it cool.

"I *knew* it! What are you going to do?" Paige was completely invested. She had a college, school-girl-style enthusiasm that Alice could get behind.

Appreciating the encouragement and the question, Alice made a mental note to do a little extra for Paige when her courses started up again. She'd still see her in the mornings, but she'd miss her during those afternoons when Paige would be running through campus in crewneck sweaters and driving the boys wild.

Paige had become the little sister Alice didn't even know she wanted. And if Alice wasn't careful, she could get carried away appreciating the young woman. But, for now, she had a different task at hand.

"What am I going to do?" Alice repeated the question, then sighed. She really couldn't believe what she was about to say, but desperate times called for desperate measures.

"I know what I'm going to do." Alice looked Paige in the eyes and answered her own question. "I'm going to show up everywhere. I'm going to bring him coffee in the morning and a treat in the afternoon. I'm going to find out where he shops, where he lives, where he decides to go out to dinner on a Friday night." Alice bobbed her head back and forth, realizing what she just said.

Paige nodded and shrugged before they both admitted, "The diner."

It really was the only place for him to go.

"But." Alice got back on track. "I am going to make it so he can't ignore me and can't run away." Her determined fist found the top of the counter.

Then Alice looked down, pausing for a moment before saying, "All of that actually sounded a little stalker-y, didn't it?"

"I mean, only a little." Paige tried her best to assure Alice she wasn't crazy. "But I *love* the enthusiasm. Really going for what you want." Paige added a supportive fist pump to accompany her encouragement.

"A little stalker-y," Alice repeated.

"Yeah, maybe a little." Paige couldn't deny it.

"Or, maybe a lot."

Alice and Paige looked up to see Beck and Riley walk through the door. They'd been so into their gossip they hadn't even heard the chime. Riley was smiling ear-to-ear at her comment on Alice's plan of action.

"Hey, it's a small town. Running into people isn't weird." Alice defended herself.

Paige tied her hair back and offered Alice a supportive smile before walking to the front of the shop to prep the area for customers.

Riley nodded when Paige was out of sight. "Right, I suppose it's not like you put a trace on him – which would actually make your life a lot easier."

"Nope, no magic. I'm doing this the good old-fashioned way. Hunt him down and make him want me."

"Right. That doesn't sound scary at all," Riley said.

"It's not," Beck chimed in and held out a piece of paper for Alice. "Because she has a schedule. No hunting necessary."

Alice's eyes grew hungry with hope and all the possibilities that one tiny little paper – holding every minute of Theo's daily agenda – offered her.

"I'm not a stalker!" Alice cheered. "Thank you!"

Beck waved a hand that said it was no big deal, then she added, "We'll review the definition of *stalker* later. But for now, I'm all in on this. I love a good love story."

"Let's not get ahead of ourselves." Alice laughed self-consciously and started tugging at her hair with her spare hand.

Please. Beck shot her thoughts into Alice and Riley's minds when she heard Paige humming around outside the door. *I felt the way your heart pounded all the way next door when he pulled into town. You know what that means.*

Alice paused, unblinking. Then she shifted her eyes from Beck to Riley – who was already rolling her eyes.

Riley folded her arms and looked at Beck. *She doesn't know what that means.*

Beck lifted her eyebrows in surprise and gave Alice a questioning look, wondering if she really didn't know what all this meant. *She really doesn't know,* Beck thought, primarily to herself.

I really don't know! Tell me what you're talking about. Alice's mind shouted at her cousins.

Beck gave Riley a knowing look. *She needs the–*

Don't. You. Dare. Alice squinted at Beck, knowing what she was about to think.

All the while, Riley couldn't have been more satisfied.

"So, naturally, you're going to start today, right?"

Alice, Beck, and Riley turned their heads to Paige, who had walked back in on the three of them. She didn't seem to think anything of what probably looked to her like an insane staring contest. Instead, she just joined right back in on the conversation.

Alice stomped her tall brown riding boot for effect. "Yes." She lifted the paper filled with the details of Theo's day and confirmed, "today is the day."

CHAPTER 6

Before taking off for the day, Alice needed to make sure all of their syrups and spices were stocked for Paige to use until they closed that afternoon. Then, because the time allowed – and because she had the comfort of knowing Theo wouldn't be in the office until eight – she reviewed her own agenda book and hovered the floating pen over the following Saturday.

Should I go? Should I not go?

Alice rested her head on her hands. Then, with her face level with the pen that was now drawing lazy circles around Saturday all by itself, she blew out a breath.

The shrill of Alice's phone startled her, and the pen fell to the desk. She fumbled for it after her elbow had knocked it toward the edge of the desk.

"Hello?" she answered, breathless from the surprise.

Alice immediately regretted rushing to answer and not checking the caller ID upon hearing the voice on the other end.

"Alice! Dear!" Clementine's old scratchy voice sang through the phone. "We were all sitting here, and all of a sudden, we knew we had to call."

We meant…

"Hello, darling!" Parsnip's screeching inflection filled the receiver.

Then Peach offered her excited greeting. "Good morning, Alice!"

She loved them – she *really* did. But her aunts were a little…eccentric. They really embraced their witch culture, their history, and their powers.

In fact, Alice wondered if they were even talking to her through a telephone. Usually, it was through a hole they formed in the center of a circle. Because it was either that or the less likely scenario: they'd figured out how to use the speaker on their phone.

And the only thing worse than an over-magic'd trio of crazy aunts was the constant and insistent way they meddled.

And, they meddled in *everything.*

Everything from who should be mayor of the town to what the diner special should be on a Thursday night. Total abuse of power – especially when it came to…

"Now, Alice, tell us about this man," Clementine said on cue, perfectly proving the point Alice's mind was trying to make.

She tried to lie. "There is no man."

"Honey," Peach cut in. "We felt it, too. Best to just come on out with it."

Alice dropped her face into her hand. "It's a…work in progress." She knew the words sounded muffled.

"What do you mean *work in progress*? *He* felt it, too."

Parsnip obviously hadn't felt the aftermath of Theo repeating the word *No* at the sight of her and then running away. But perhaps some things were better left untold. And if Alice was honest with herself, though he was highly adorable at that moment, she didn't overly like the idea of him basically running away from her.

"He did?" Alice asked, finally letting Parsnip's words sink in. She hadn't been able to read him, or see, or feel anything about him. Only the way her own heart had sped up, then came to a crashing halt.

Alice listened as the whispering started.

She can't see. That's unusual. She should have paid more attention in training. It's an interesting conundrum.

"Stop." Alice broke up the pow-wow. "What can't I see? And what's a conundrum?" She hated that her curiosity had been stronger than her resolve. Because they knew they had her.

"We'll see you Saturday, honey. Talk then." Peach signed off for the gaggle of them before a puff of purple-gray smoke curled away from Alice's phone.

Well, at least she knew they still didn't know how to use the speaker on their phone. But the humor in it wasn't a comfort at the moment. Apparently, there was some sort of hiccup when it came to Theo. And worse than that, she needed to go to her aunts on Saturday.

Alice let the mindless work of mixing potions fill her time nicely. She smoothly ordered spell poems while billowy clouds of smoke bubbled over her new cauldron. When the potions were mixed, Alice filled large syrup bottles with the liquid that would help her customers with confidence, baldness, or love. For any need, she had a drink.

Speaking of, she wondered how Blanche and Tom were holding up?

The thought went as quickly as it came, as Alice focused on creating spice packets for tea that would help with ailments, energy, or sleep. Really, all of what she mixed up was *mostly* natural. But she had a knack for enhancing recipes provided by Mother Nature into potions with the simple flick of a wrist, a quick charm, or a bewitching spell.

Usually, she wouldn't allow for such a public use of witchery, but all of what she did was used for good. Her potions helped people.

By the time she'd carried the new potions – that were expertly covert in their pump bottles and tea spice jars – and stocked them in the storage room of the coffee shop, it was time for her to get started on the real matter at hand: how to make Theo Parker fall in love with her.

Step one: *Talk to him.*

Alice let her head fall back, and the long red curls dangle in their binder. The amusement of the situation was not lost on her. She had seen him once, dreamt of him twice, and she wanted him to love her? If those were the only prerequisites to love, the entire world would be in trouble.

But this was different. And she needed to find out why.

"Now." Alice looked at Grumbles. He had relocated to the storage room to be with her when the chaos from the customers started interfering with his nap. "All I need to do is find that agenda from Beck."

Alice spun in a circle, and by the time she found her way around, Grumbles was sitting up with it in his mouth.

"Right. Thank you." Alice bent over, touched her head to his, and massaged both of his ears. Then took the paper from his soggy lips. She dried the slobber with a quick blow of air and looked down.

"Hmmm," she said, eyeing the smudge where the drool had erased the appointment times.

Alice lifted a single brow and looked down in Grumbles' direction, who had already plopped at her feet. "I suppose we could just start at the top and work our way down. Eventually, we'd run into him, right?"

Grumbles lifted his head and raised his brows right back at Alice. Then, he tilted his head to relay his unspoken message. *Did you say we?*

Alice put her hands on her hips. "Yes, *we*. You're my wingman. You know I need you."

Resigned, Grumbles pushed off the floor with his front legs, then his back. Finally, he stretched and let out a tired moan but turned to face the door.

"That's my boy. Okay," Alice said, eyeing the schedule. "First stop, office meeting. Let's bring lattes for the crew."

CHAPTER 7

The wind swirled some crisp leaves around Theo as he exited his apartment and started his stroll into work. Aside from feeling like he hadn't gotten a wink of sleep since he spent all night avoiding Alice in his dreams, he was excited for the day.

He would have a new office, new rules, new scenery – he was ready. Even the idea of getting out and meeting the townspeople, learning the landscape, what happened down at the harbor – all of it was energizing.

Theo was yearning for a latte, but he wasn't ready to come face-to-face with a woman he reluctantly had feelings for – whom he was constantly reminding himself he'd never even met.

If *that* wasn't some kind of sorcery, he didn't know what was.

In fact, it was insane. Theo just needed to reel in that insanity and get a grip because it made him feel like he belonged in the loony bin.

"You got this. You don't need a beautiful red-headed woman." Theo picked up his pace to keep time with his pep-talk. "You are a strong, confident, and darn-it, you're a good-lookin' man. You'll get back out there when you're good and ready."

"You got that right!" An old lady sitting on the bench outside of the book store pulled her glasses down to check Theo out by squinting her eyes up and down the length of his body. "You come on back here when you're ready, young man."

Embarrassed, Theo dipped his head, let out a fake cough, and hurried the words, "Ah, thanks," as he realized he'd been talking out loud. But, it was good to know at least one person agreed with his assessment – even if she was bordering on ninety years old.

Theo shoved his hands in his pockets and walked a bit taller. Nothing like a good, self-assured stride to prove to himself he had everything under control. But just for the sake of self-preservation, he sprinted across the front windows of Witches' Brew, then resumed his walk, right into his new workplace.

Upon arrival, Theo didn't get a chance to make a casual, breezy entry. Instead, he barely had time to get his second foot through the door before he was mauled by a giant, brown bear of a dog. The low, lazy *woof* accompanied two humongous paws that pinned Theo against the door that had closed behind him.

Before Theo had a chance to duck, block, or say *no,* the dog was lapping at his face in long, sloppy licks from chin to forehead. The most Theo could do was close his mouth and hold his breath. He wouldn't let a dog be the first thing he kissed since breaking up with his ex. *No. Way.*

"Grumbles!" Beck's voice called from Lane's office. "No! Down!"

Theo noticed her voice seemed more urgent than her stride.

Don't worry about me, he thought sarcastically as he started laughing at the hilarity – and the grossness – of the moment.

"Sorry," Beck said as she hurried her way over to the scene of the sloppy make-out session. She used her whole body – that weighed less than the dog – to pull the animal off of him. "He doesn't usually get that friendly with people."

"Friendly?" Theo asked while laughing on his way down to a kneel to scratch the dog's ears and run fingers over his head. "I feel like he was about to round second base."

"Yeah, well, I can't comment on the base coverage." Beck grinned. "But I can tell you he's the best dog I know. And his person is the best I know. Grumbles wouldn't do anything his owner wouldn't do. *Would you, sweet big boy?"* Beck's last question was directed at the dog in perfected baby-talk.

Theo stared for an extra second after he swore he saw the dog nod.

Wouldn't do anything the owner wouldn't do. Theo chuckled at the comment and mindlessly thought: *Well if that's the case, I hope it's a woman.*

When Theo looked up, he saw a dangerously amused look on Beck's face.

"What is it?" Theo asked with a tentative grin.

"I feel like I'm being rude, introducing Grumbles and not his owner. But I think you two have crossed paths. Theo," Beck slid sideways, so she wasn't blocking the view, "this is Alice. She belongs to Grumbles. She wanted to bring you a drink on your first day. Isn't that wonderful?"

"Ahh." Words escaped him.

Theo stood, mouth open, dragging out the dumbfounded sound at the vision of the woman standing before him. He tried to pinpoint what it was about her that left him speechless – no, thoughtless – but it seemed to be everything.

Was it the intriguing way her piercing blue eyes looked as if they were trying to bore into his soul? Was it the magnificent way her cheekbones sat impossibly high on her face, or the way her nose sloped into a dainty point? Or, maybe it was the dusting of freckles that gave her cheeks a bit of color, then scattered and spread across a bright, pale face?

Whatever it was, it was bewitching.

"I'm Alice." Alice reached out her hand and let it hover in front of Theo.

Theo looked down at it briefly as if he had no idea what to do with it, then looked back at her face that was sporting an amused grin.

Beck leaned forward a bit, ushering Theo closer to Alice's hand. "And this is," Beck started as if guiding Theo into the words he couldn't find or say.

Theo stole a look at Beck, who was nodding to him and mouthing his name, encouraging him to speak it out loud.

Theo began nodding with her, and when Beck's mouth formed the word, he said, "Theo." He nodded more, looking forward. Then as if he was excited that he remembered his name, he repeated, "Theo Parker."

Then he took her hand.

A gust of wind encircled them, spinning so forcefully it pushed Alice and Theo closer to one another. Inside, Theo felt the attraction to Alice amplify, like it became the electricity to his mind and his body. He looked down to see if he *looked* different and saw nothing.

Was he hallucinating? Going crazy? Still dreaming?

Alice held eye contact, unmoving, while Theo looked around, wondering if the others were seeing this – feeling this – or if he was losing his mind.

When Alice broke their connection, the wind evaporated, and the lightness in his body felt the weight of gravity once more. Like everything fell back into its usual, boring place.

"So, Theo," Beck started, drawing his attention to her cute grin, "why don't we get you settled at your new desk? Maybe Alice would like to join us for lunch?"

"No!" Theo bellowed the rejection, like a desperate, pubescent teenager. His entire audience jumped at the volume and the sharp refusal. Even Grumbles moaned and pouted his way down into a lying position on the floor.

"Whoa, buddy," Lane said from his desk, looking around, surprised at the outburst, "we just thought it would be nice to meet some new people in town."

Theo tried to back-pedal. "No. Sorry, I mean, I just don't want to be a bother. I figure there's so much you probably have to do and that I have to do. You know?"

Theo begged his brain for an example. "Like, count the steps from here to the harbor. Time the distance from our office to different locations in town. Probably check out any handbooks you have on policies and procedures. All that stuff. So, no." Theo looked around at the big, amused faces staring back at him. "No, thank you," he corrected as if it made his ridiculous tirade saner.

"Well," Alice said, "if you need anything at all, I'm just next door." She moved a step toward the door, and Theo jumped backward.

"I'm just going to–" Theo pointed to the back office, then walked in the direction of his finger.

Beck and Alice stared after Theo until he was out of sight, then turned to Lane, who looked like he had no idea what had just happened to his friend. "I'm going to, ah, do that, too. To check on him. Because that was…strange."

When Lane and Theo were safely behind the closed door of Lane's office, Alice threw herself around to look Beck straight on. "Did you see that? Tell me you saw that."

Beck widened her eyes. Not surprised or in shock. Instead, she was impressed by the magical forces at play. "Oh, I saw it."

"There's no way we *act* like it actually happened, though, right?" Alice wondered if she should try and explain herself to Theo.

"Yeah, we definitely don't say anything. I think maybe let's just let Theo have a moment. Or a day. Or two. Until Theo can make an excuse as to why he went crazy for five full seconds. I'm sure he'll be fine."

"He didn't look fine," Alice admitted.

"How do you feel?" Beck felt like she didn't have to agree that Theo looked like he felt just as crazy as the whole scenario seemed.

Alice took a deep breath. "Honestly?"

"That's usually a good place to start," Beck reassured.

"Like I'm in love with a man who I don't know and who I'm pretty sure is terrified of me. He shouted–"

"Yeah, I know," Beck stepped in, agreeing with Alice, so she wouldn't have to say the words out loud. Sometimes magic did funny things when a witch didn't have complete control over her feelings. It was best to keep things inside and unsaid during those moments. "Maybe it's best if you go back to Witches' Brew for the day."

"But you saw us. It's powerful. I *have* to see him. I *have* to know him. Like I've never wanted to know another person before. He's…perfect." Alice felt the hint of lunacy that tinged her words. Then she nodded. "I should go."

"Just for a day…or two." Beck put a comforting hand on Alice's arm. "By the way, you look fabulous today."

"Thanks." Alice shrugged. "I tried," she admitted, pointing to the back of the office where Theo was currently hiding from her to indicate that *he* was the reason she looked like she did. A premeditated approach to wooing a man.

CHAPTER 8

"It's harder than I thought it would be." Alice paced back and forth down the length of the romance section in Riley's book shop.

"Come again?" Riley asked as she used her hands to carefully rearrange the new books that had been delivered. Each of them hovered over a shelf before she waved a hand or flicked a wrist to push it in.

"You can read my mind. And you're still going to make me say it?" Alice asked dryly as she stopped her pacing.

"Sorry, yeah. Your mind is jumbled right now. It's hard getting in there," Beck admitted.

Alice bobbed her head, accepting the truth. In fact, it was probably more than jumbled. It was like a hurricane of thoughts, emotions, indescribable and unrealistic longing, and love. Of all things – *freaking love.*

Alice shook her head to shake the last thought from it. "Meeting Theo. Theo Parker." Alice took a moment to swoon. "Isn't his name just perfect? And isn't *he* just perfect?"

Alice crossed her feet at the ankles, and in one fluid motion, dropped herself to the floor, so she was sitting cross-legged next to Riley. Her face took on a dreamy gaze, and her eyes turned to mush. "You know, I can't even see inside of him, and I just *know* he's the one. I can *feel* that he's nice, and funny, and good."

"But you were saying earlier…something about it being hard?" Riley tried to get her nuts-and-in-love friend back on track.

"Oh, right. I mean, I know I've never really been interested in anybody before or tried to pursue a man – or a woman. Sure, I've dated, it's been nice, but now that I feel like I want to – no – *need* to, it's tough."

Riley wondered if Alice remembered all of their years growing up together? All of the boys – young and old – who tried to lure Alice into their hearts – or beds. But Alice simply went on being perfectly oblivious and driving crazy for it.

"What would you do?" Alice finally asked when Riley hadn't said anything.

"Me?" Riley stuttered, getting caught off guard. "Um, I guess I would probably…talk to him?"

Alice paid no mind to Riley's advice coming out in the form of a question. To her, it was brilliant. "Riley! That's *exactly* what I need to do. I mean, how hard can that possibly be?"

For a normal person? Or you?

"Hey, I heard that." Alice folded her arms.

"Sorry, no, you're right. You should talk to Theo." Riley supported her earlier lackadaisical advice. But after what Beck had told her happened earlier that day in the Sheriff's office, getting Theo and Alice to have a civilized conversation might be the hardest thing either of them might ever have to do. Between the tornadoes and the stuttering, it might be impossible.

"I still think you should talk to the–"

"I know. I'm going, okay?" Alice didn't want to hear another person say *the aunts*. But, if they could give her answers, she'd take whatever lecture was waiting for her upon her next visit.

Riley rolled her eyes playfully. Alice didn't have to be as scared of the aunts as she was. As kooky as they were, they all meant well. And, because they embraced their witchcraft, they were definitely the ones to go to when you were in trouble – and from what Riley was seeing in her friend, there were some strange powers at play. And she'd never seen her friend quite as determined as she was today. The next couple of weeks were definitely going to be interesting.

"Hey." Alice lifted herself off the floor. "What are you doing Friday night?"

Riley grinned. "What did you have in mind?"

"I've got a hankering for new beverages. What do you say? Are you in for a night of drinks and desserts?"

Riley leaned her head back, dreaming of how good a night in, fire blazing, warm drinks brewing, and desserts getting devoured sounded to her.

"Yes. And can I just say, I'm so happy we are over the age of tricks and can focus more on the treats?"

"Not even my spellbook could have said it better. See you at seven?" Alice asked.

"In my sweats and slippers."

"It's a date."

"So, what are you up to this afternoon?" Riley stood and linked her arm with Alice's as they started to walk back toward the center of the store.

Alice beamed as if her day was perfectly planned and would go on without a hitch.

"It's going to be so fun! I'm going to bring an afternoon treat to Theo. Maybe he'll even talk to me this time."

Riley's eyebrows lifted at the naïve idea her friend came up with. "Right. Already," Riley deadpanned. "I can't see at all how that could go terribly wrong."

Not listening to the sarcasm or paying attention to anything but the words, Alice agreed, "I know, right? It's going to be great."

CHAPTER 9

Theo and Lane had driven a cruiser down a curvy road toward the harbor. When they reached the beginning of a long boardwalk that lined the edge of the water, they parked and hopped out.

They could have driven, but Lane liked the walk, taking in the small boats that came in and out of port and the little shaker-framed shacks that sat across the road offering people a place to eat the day's catch, clean fish, rent boats, or grab a beer.

The wind from the water whipped around the men, but rather than find it uncomfortable, Theo thought it only added to the autumn appeal. Something about the gray sky that hovered over this part of the town, the way the leaves took on a dull-rustic color, and the way everybody who wandered the boardwalk with them were bundled in jackets, hats, and scarves made him feel outdoorsy. All he needed was a giant insulated mug of coffee and a fishing pole, and he'd be set for the day.

"Do you ever fish down here?" Theo decided to ask the question out loud to Lane while shoving his chilled hands in his pockets.

Lane lifted one side of his mouth in a knowing grin. "Already trying to get an angle on the good spots, huh?"

Theo laughed a little and shrugged. "Seems like the manly thing to do when presented with gusty winds and some water."

"Once you go fishing, you'll never want to leave. The catch here is the best I've ever known."

Lane nodded ahead, and Theo's eyes followed. "At the end of the boardwalk, there's a dirt path that veers left. It travels along the edge of the water. Once you get into the wooded area, there's a small peak that hovers over the water – about five feet above the water. When I drop a line in there, I never go home empty-handed."

Theo nodded, appreciating the insight.

Lane saw the nod, looked forward, then did a double-take back to Theo.

"What?" Theo asked, feeling the unasked question.

"I just–" Lane didn't quite know what to say.

"Come on, out with it."

"Alice," Lane said only her name, and the reaction it caused in Theo was exactly why he was going to ask the question.

Theo's head shot forward and at just the name of the woman who had bewitched him since he came into town caused his heart to do its rapid pounding routine.

"*That,*" Lane said. "Exactly that – what just happened? Buddy, I hate to tell you this, but you kind of give the weirdo vibe. Here, when I just say her name. But when she was in the office…that was a *whole* other level."

"I don't know what to do," Theo said, not knowing what to say either.

"Um, is there anything *to do?"* Lane asked, wondering what exactly Theo felt he needed to do.

"I want to marry her!"

The minute the words were out, Theo froze. His face looked like a contorted jack-o-lantern, and his mind was about as hallow as one too. His eyes bugged out of their sockets in surprise and – if he were being honest with himself – fear. Then his head slowly made the turn to look at Lane, who had been kind enough to stay silent for the moment.

"Yup," Lane said, "I wouldn't know what to do either. Especially with the whole *avoiding women* schpeel you gave me a few days ago."

Theo nodded, remembering the conversation as clear as the port water was a murky-colored gray.

Still nodding, Theo said, "I know what I have to do."

Lane nodded with him. Then they both spoke at the same time.

Only Lane said, "Talk to her."

And, Theo said, "Hide."

CHAPTER 10

"Hey, Bea!" Alice chirped happily as she all but skipped into her friend's boat shop. "What's the good word from the water?"

Beatrice was the sandy-haired blonde that basically ran the entire harbor as a one-woman show. She came to work every day with a long braid, a flat felt hat that shielded her face from the sun and her head from the cold, and green or black rubber wellies – depending on the outfit she chose for the day. She constantly moved and broke the hearts of merchant owners, townspeople, captains, and fishermen alike.

"Back here!"

Alice smiled at the yell and at the stream of curse words she could hear filling Bea's mind. Why say them aloud if they delivered the same sense of purpose in your head – and when fellow witches could still appreciate them?

When Alice stepped through the door behind the register and ship log station, she found Bea man-handling – or fighting – with a fishnet that nearly doubled the size of the tall blonde.

Alice leaned against the door and grinned. "Want some help?"

No. The silent words shot in Alice's direction.

"I know I'm not the one to tout the use of the M-word, but you could use – dare I say it," Alice turned her voice to a whisper for the humor of it and her surroundings. *"Magic."*

Bea grunted the net across the cement floor toward an open garage bay at the back end of the building, then dropped it in the middle of the opening. She took a deep breath to help catch the ones she lost in the struggle and finally looked up with her long hands on her hips.

"I'm ignoring you," Beatrice said, then turned her flat face into a smile.

"I gathered that much." Alice smiled back.

"What are you doing down here? Shouldn't you be curing life's issues for the townspeople of Lantern Lane?" Beatrice took long strides back toward the front and followed Alice into the shop side of her store.

Alice shrugged casually, waited for a beat, then hurried to the counter to hover over it. "I'm meeting a guy here."

Surprised, Bea leaned on the counter herself. She wasn't one to take part in town gossip, but this was big news. Unlike Bea, Alice had been single her entire life. "Can you say that one more time for me? I'm not sure I heard that right."

Alice nudged her shoulder into Bea's. "He's *the one."*

"Wow. I had no idea. How long have you known him?" Beatrice asked, wondering if her friend, and cousin, had been keeping a secret from her.

"I've known *of* him for two days. I've officially *known* him, for one. And–"

"Whoa, whoa. Hold on. Did you just say you've known *of* him for two days?" Bea asked, adding the necessary dramatic effect to the length of time to show essential surprise at how ridiculous that sounded.

"Yes." Alice looked confused. "Are my thoughts and words getting mixed up again?" Alice wondered aloud, knowing that sometimes it was hard to listen to both simultaneously – especially in her current situation.

"Oh, no. I heard you."

"Oh, then why do you ask?" Alice asked as if everything was completely normal.

"I know that being a part of the witching world often lends to some strange situations and scenarios," Bea started. "But, ah, when you say he's *the one*, and then follow it up with you've known *of him for two days*, it doesn't really scream sanity if you know what I mean?"

"I know, right?" Alice mused as if she had wholly accepted her totally illogical situation. "It's all *very* new."

"You can say that again," Bea said the words mostly to herself.

"It's all thundering heartbeats, tornadoes inside the Sheriff's office, Grumbles basically making out with him, and do you want to know the strangest part?" Alice asked, enraptured by her own story.

"Ah, yes. I definitely think after all of that I'm entitled to know what you find stranger than all of…well, that."

"I can't read him. At all." Alice flattened her hands to indicate her ability to read Theo's mind.

"Huh." Bea had to admit that was a little strange. Tapping into another person's thoughts was one of the simpler things to do. It mainly required focus and surprisingly little magic. Non-magical people could do it if they paid enough attention. And twins? They did it all the time. "Have you tried talking to the aunts?"

Alice stared and blinked for the amount of time it would have taken her to try and stop Bea from suggesting she visit *the aunts*.

"What?" Bea asked, oblivious to the annoyance.

Alice sighed. "Never mind. And yes. I mean no. I haven't talked to the aunts. But yes, I'm going."

"That's great. So, I'll see you Saturday then?" Bea seemed excited about the idea.

How was it that Bea, a witch who rarely used her powers, was unaffected by the onslaught of the aunt's badgering?

"Yes," Alice said blandly as if it was going to ruin her entire fall season by going.

Bea grinned. "So, this guy? He's meeting you here?"

"Kind of."

"Now I'm a little confused," Bea admitted.

"Well, it's really not that confusing. Beck gave me his schedule. He's going to be here any minute, so I thought I'd bring him an apple popover from Franny's."

"You're stalking him," Bea said as she stood upright when the old brass boat bell that hung above her door clanged. Bea's eyes narrowed as she watched the bearded, sasquatch of a man walk through.

"I'm not," Alice argued, then asked a question of her own while nodding to the tall man who came through the door. "Friend of yours?"

The sarcasm wasn't lost on Beatrice. "I could have a hundred people come through here on any given day. They are nice or nice enough to stay quiet. This guy? Every time he complains that there aren't Twinkies. *Twinkies!*" Bea emphasized the absurdity of the snack.

"We have homemade pumpkin bars, mini apple pies, pecan caramel rolls, and those are just the okay-tasting snacks. And he wants *Twinkies!*"

Alice pinched her lips together so she wouldn't smile, but it didn't quite stop the humor from reaching her eyes. "I know I'm not really in the *sane bucket* these days, but would it be totally crazy to just, you know, stock Twinkies?"

The speed at which Bea's wide eyes found Alice's was answer enough.

"Okay." Alice stepped aside so the man could move to the counter.

She decided to sit back and watch what she hoped would be a fun exchange play out in front of her.

Alice thought she could offer some assistance when Bea stood with her arms folded on the opposite side of the counter from the man doing nothing.

"What do you have there?" she asked, leaning over the counter a bit to see that he'd selected a pumpkin Danish with cream cheese frosting drizzle.

The man looked over. He took inventory of the woman who asked the question. He'd seen her around before but didn't care enough to make conversation. He decided, though beautiful, she was probably harmless. "Had to pick the pumpkin thing."

"It sounds like you're disappointed?" Alice offered a smile with her probing question.

"It ain't a Twinkie," the man responded while burning his disapproving eyes into Bea.

"I'm sorry, I'm sure I've seen you around," Alice began, more interested in the man Bea seemed to loathe by the second. "But, I've never caught your name."

"Mack. Name's Mack."

"Nice to meet you, Mack. I'm Alice Balfour. This is Beatrice Proctor. But, it does look like you already know each other."

"Yeah," Mack huffed. "We know each other."

Alice noted Mack didn't seem thrilled about the situation.

With an unmoving Beatrice, Mack finally gave in. Like blinking first in a staring contest. He didn't speak, just pushed his Danish and soda pop bottles farther onto the counter.

Feeling Alice's eyes and her laughing thoughts, Bea reluctantly started to move. She entered the prices of the items by hand into the old metal register, not bothering to bag the items.

It seemed to be the routine.

Mack pointedly grabbed each one and shoved them into the snug pockets of his fisherman's pants. Then, with a bit more ease, he pushed the Danish into his jacket pocket.

Mack lingered.

Then after an irritated huff, Bea finally spoke. "The nets are out back. Close the door when you're done."

Mack nodded and started toward the door. He stopped short of it as if contemplating his next move. Without turning around, he said, "It's stalking." Then pushed his way out of the door.

Deciding to push her dislike of Mack aside for three seconds, Bea sent a satisfied grin to Alice, who was now furrowing her auburn eyebrows in the direction of the door.

"You're right," Alice said, "he's *not* a good man."

KATIE BACHAND

CHAPTER 11

Theo and Lane had made their way down a long dock and introduced themselves to some of the regulars who rented boat slips, then they walked along the shops to talk to the owners or the townspeople that came down to the water for an afternoon snack.

The last place they were scheduled to walk into was a wood-paneled building that looked more like a small cabin than a boardwalk shop.

The weathered wooden sign that hung above the shop swayed back and forth on two chains and told Theo they were walking into *The Boat Shop.*

"This is Beatrice Proctor's store. Everybody calls her Bea. She manages the ship log and any goods coming in or out of Lantern Lane. Has supplies in the back room – mostly for the fishermen. And she makes a killing for the diner selling their pastries and pies to the hungry guys that come to shore. It's a good little market."

Theo listened to the heavy clank of the bell just above him as he walked into the shop. He was pleasantly surprised to find it didn't smell like fish. It smelled like river water and fallen leaves.

And, if he wasn't mistaken, he smelled the treats from the diner Lane had just told him about. If he hadn't had a job to do, he would have marched right down the first aisle toward the bakery stand along the sidewall of the shop.

"Theo Parker," Bea said from the stool she'd perched herself on as she ran through her port logs for the day. There was no doubt this was the man Alice was waiting for. "Aren't you a sight for sore eyes?"

Theo smiled as he took in yet another magnificent face. This one, still beautiful, but rather than narrow, sharp angles like Alice, Bea had a lean square face with a straight up and down frame. She looked like the farmer's daughter who'd been plucked out of the field and plopped on the river's edge and traded her work boots for tall water shoes.

Fascinating.

Bea grinned at the internal assessment Theo had given her on his approach. She also noted he didn't seem even the slightest bit interested in her beyond the intrigue of the women he'd crossed paths with thus far. Of course, he hadn't been there long, but what Bea found the most fascinating was his determined avoidance of Alice. It's like his mind was actively trying to *not* think of her. And, as much as he tried not to, the fireworks were sparking just below the surface.

Yeah, Alice needed the aunts. Bea had never seen anything like it.

"Good news travels fast." Theo offered a casual smile.

You have no idea. Bea thought. "How's your first day?"

"Have to admit, the town has the sort of appeal that makes a guy want to stick around."

"You're not planning on staying?" Bea asked, wondering if Alice knew that small detail about the man she'd claimed was *the one.*

Theo rubbed at his jawline. It felt like home from the moment he drove in. But he knew he couldn't stay. He was only here long enough to put his life back together. "No. No plans to stay long term. Just helping out an old friend."

"I think he's going to stay." Lane walked up behind Theo, showing a smile full of teeth and dipping his sheriff's hat toward Bea. "How's it going, Bea?"

"Pretty good. Hey, you guys are just in time. Alice stopped by with some popovers from the diner."

"No, ah, no thanks." Theo tried to backpedal while he wondered if Alice had decided to haunt more than his dreams.

"Hey, Alice!" Bea shouted toward the back. "Why don't you bring out some of those popovers. Lane and Theo Parker are here visiting." Bea blatantly ignored Theo's decline.

When Alice swung through the door, Theo held his breath so the agonizing blow to his gut from the rapture of the woman he was about to see wouldn't knock him over.

"Hey, Lane. Hey, Theo. What a crazy coincidence," Alice said while ignoring the sarcastic thoughts from Bea, who was singing *stalker!* in her mind.

"Alice, these smell great," Lane said, taking a step toward the box in Alice's hand. "I'd love one if you have enough to spare."

"It's all for you."

Liar.

Alice darted her eyes at Bea, who was having way too much fun with her situation.

"Theo, it's good seeing you again." Alice offered her hand, but Theo jumped to the side, avoiding it like his survival depended on it. Alice tried to keep her smile.

Rather than let the twinge of hurt show, she raised the box so he could peer over the side.

Unable to resist the scent of buttery, cinnamon, and sugar apples. And the appealing look of the popovers, Theo slowly reached his hand inside, careful to touch nothing but the popover. He refused to have a repeat of the storm that nearly knocked him out of his work boots that morning.

"How's your first day?" Alice asked, more than satisfied at the progress they were making in such a short amount of time. The day before, he'd run from her. This morning she'd gotten about five seconds worth of tornado along with an emergency exit from him. And as soon as this afternoon, he was accepting popovers from her. She might be able to tell him she loved him much sooner than anticipated.

Absolutely not!

Beatrice's eyes bored into Alice along with her passionate plea for Alice *not* to confess her love to Theo.

Alice gave her a look like a teenager pleading with a parent who just didn't understand what she was going through.

Why not?

Bea panicked, wondering how much she should tell her friend. Bea sat back, staring at Alice, wondering how much she could take.

During the stare-off, Theo side-stepped his way toward Lane and whispered through an admittedly delectable bite of apple popover, "Is it just me, or do some of the women here seem different?"

Theo didn't quite know how to describe the women he'd met thus far or how they interacted. There were a lot of wide eyes and furrowed eyebrows.

Lane shrugged and whispered back. "They are women. They can read each other's minds." Lane had accepted the notion upon moving to Lantern Lane that women were magical. They knew your thoughts, actions, what you wanted to do, and what you *should* do before you even knew what you were thinking. He was an intelligent man, but women, he knew, were smarter.

He's blocking you out. Bea finally sent the thought over to Alice.

Alice gasped, then smiled, remembering they had an audience.

"Well," she tried to recover. "I better get back up to the coffee shop. We've got lots of thirsty people to serve. Lots of issues to resolve. You know?" Alice blabbered, hoping she didn't sound insane. "Headaches, backaches, heartaches. So, I'll just see you all around then."

Alice tested a small step in Theo's direction before walking to the door and tried not to let his retreat affect her.

"See you around. Nice to see you again, Theo."

I'm sorry.

Alice listened to Bea's thoughts and sent one of her own. *I'm not worried. He's going to love me back.*

She didn't mean it as a threat but rather as a premonition or the next logical step: he *would* come to feel what she felt. She knew she probably sounded crazy to everyone else – even to herself – but she had never felt this kind of gravitational pull toward anyone or anything before.

However, she had to admit that the rejection in the meantime stung. And it was becoming a bit annoying.

Theo didn't realize he'd been holding his breath as he watched Alice move to a safer distance and head for the door. He slowly brought the apple popover to his mouth for another bite.

On her way out, Alice flicked her wrist. And as Theo took a bite, his hand pushed the popover into his face.

"Oh dear," Bea said, trying to keep her lips in a straight line and not curve with the giggle she was trying hard to hold inside.

The shock on Theo's face was enough to make anybody laugh – and Lane did – to the point where he was no help at all.

"Here you go," Bea said as she offered Theo a stack of napkins. As she watched Theo wipe his face clean was; *This poor guy, he has no idea what he's gotten himself into.*

CHAPTER 12

Alice was coming off of a night filled with laughter, warm drinks, and desserts with her best friend in the world, so on Saturday morning, she was already in a good mood.

Then she was able to spend the rest of the morning walking through town with Grumbles, casually showing up where Theo was while carefully staying out of sight. It didn't make her a stalker. She was simply enjoying the lovely crisp air, warm sun, and vibrant fall colors that decorated her surroundings.

Occasionally she used a bit of magic to help her hide or to help Theo with something he was doing – from afar, of course.

Even when Alice had arrived at Willa's farm, she was in good spirits - and she was handed one upon arrival. The old farmhouse was antique and adorable, but the sort of mother-in-law suite that housed her aunts was a different story. Even in the pretty gray-blue of the evening and the dewy, foggy hue that settled over the farm and fields, the aunt's house looked like a rickety, haunted, ramshackle building.

Even so, with the lovely day she'd had, and now while holding a pretty pomegranate drink, her anxiety was low, and she was feeling ready for the magical night that lay ahead.

Though she had anticipated a feeling of dread. So any emotion other than terror was a broomstick pointed in the right direction.

But when Alice found herself in the middle of a circle with her crazy aunts chanting their own part of a spell – looking and sounding like rambling lunatics - her mood quickly took a plunge.

While her cousins and friends were sipping more *spirits*, grinning from ear-to-ear, *she* was being cloaked with a safety blanket. Which looked an awful lot like dark gray smoke that billowed around her head and caused a coughing jig from time to time.

Alice sat cross-legged as a fire started to crackle from the broomsticks holding her captive inside the circle. The candles in the room started flickering, but no one seemed to mind since all that meant was whatever the aunts were doing was working.

Alice looked up when Clementine, Parsnip, and Peach all stopped their chants at exactly the same time. The smoke seemed to suck back into wherever it mysteriously came from. And all of the aunts gasped. Well, Parsnip and Peach gasped; Clementine's noise sounded like a hairy cackle but seemed appropriate for an old, wrinkled witch.

The spectators tried not to appear too interested, but Alice noticed Riley, Beck, Bea, and Franny's posture straighten just a bit as they tried to peek into the circle where she sat. Too bad Willa was outside and missing the show. *Lucky.*

"Well?" Alice prodded when her aunts did nothing after their dramatic gasping – or choking.

"He's never going to willingly love you." Clementine finally spoke. Her words received glum nods from Parsnip and Peach.

"You can't just say that and nod around at each other." Alice felt a bit of panic rise in her. "You have to tell me *why.*"

Peach, who actually looked a lot like a peach – if peaches wore pointy black hats with matching pointy black boots – said, "Oh dear, it's nothing you've done."

"Thank you, Auntie Peach. But again, that doesn't really help me." Alice stood in the circle and spun toward the round aunt of the group.

"It's the curse, dear." Parsnip – who sounded like the stereotypical screechy witch – nodded agreement with her own words and with her sisters, who started nodding along.

"And what curse might that be?" Alice wondered why this was the first time she was hearing about a curse. And, more importantly, why was she the target.

"One second, dear," Peach said before they threw a cloud of smoke around Alice so she couldn't see or hear what the aunts were discussing.

"This is just ridiculous. *This* is exactly why I don't come to these crazy things. It's all smoke, and curses, and drinks." Alice thought for a second as she ranted to herself, then bobbed her head for nobody to see, "Well, the drinks aren't bad."

When the curtain of smoke fell away, Alice knew there was bad news. Her cousins, who now included Willa, were all staring with mouths open at what they heard the aunts just discuss.

Alice narrowed her eyes, then started to step out of the circle.

She didn't get her toe off the ground before her cousins and aunts yelled their *no's* and put up their hands to stop her from coming out.

"Somebody tell me what's going on this instant." Alice uncharacteristically stomped her foot while demanding an answer.

"We don't know if the curse is limited to you. It's quite possible it affects all of the women on Bridget's side of the family tree."

Parsnip's chortled voice had Alice wanting to clear her throat for the batty old woman. But rather than waste energy on focusing on her shrill-sounding aunt, Alice looked to her cousins. They were all their own branch on the right side of the family tree – each a distinctive odd number. That explained the concerned looks from earlier.

Peach, the expert on the family tree, began with an explanation. "You, and you all," Peach said, looking not only at Alice but turning to look at her cousins, "are fortunate to be a descendant of Bridget Bishop."

Alice waited for the comical pause as her aunts dropped their heads and paid dramatic, brief respects to their long-lost ancestor. She felt a mouse-sized sense of accomplishment by resisting the urge to roll her eyes.

"Because of what our brave *mother* went through, she revered all of us with the curse of a loveless life."

"Whoa, whoa. Hold on there." Alice lifted a finger. She had some questions before Peach rambled on. "Why is this the first time I'm–" Alice looked at her cousins, who were just as baffled as she was. "No, *we're* just hearing about this now?"

Clementine waved a worry-free hand. "Alice, I'm sure we've mentioned this to you before. What with your lackadaisical approach to your craft, I'm not surprised it wasn't retained."

Usually, Alice would have pretended to take offense to the jab. She would have shown a sliver of defiance and defended her admittedly poor study habits. It was hard to maintain *real* school, witchcraft lessons, and a decent social life. Naturally, *one* of the three was bound to suffer. And she had excelled in public school and with her friendships.

Over the years, she'd gotten by with what witchcraft she needed – hadn't she? Wasn't her entire public life devoted to making potions and delivering them in perfectly packaged paper cups and cement mugs? But, unfortunately, nobody seemed to notice that she was the only one of the gaggle to actually use magic for their livelihood.

But that wasn't the point. Alice would have remembered something like *this.*

"Ah, I'm going to have to step in here." Willa to the rescue. The most studied, practiced one of them all spoke up. "The curse was definitely *not* mentioned to us by any of you. It wasn't in any of our study books, journals, or spellbooks. I know, *I've* done the homework."

"Hmm." Parsnip thought, then nodded. "Yes, then we must have forgotten to tell you."

Sure, *now* all of her cousins were interested. This time, Alice did roll her eyes. But she was concerned for herself and her closest family members – who were also her closest friends.

"Well, there's no time like the present! How exciting that after all of these years, the curse would still hold so strongly. Just fascinating." Clementine beamed at her sisters, who were readily nodding.

"Definitely!" Peach agreed. "How long has it been?" The sphere of a woman looked up, counting in her mind loud enough for everybody to follow along.

Nineteen-sixty-nine, seventeen, eighteen, nineteen-sixty-nine. That's three hundred. Seventy-nine, eighty-nine, ninety-nine, oh-nine, nineteen – that's fifty. Twenty, twenty-one, almost twenty-two.

"Three hundred and fifty-three years." Parsnip said the math everybody had already listened to. "Just fascinating."

Alice needed to break this up. She clapped, and a ball of energy sent just a bit of a shock around the room, causing the candles to blow out only to flicker to life once more.

"This is decidedly *not* fascinating!" Alice said once she had everybody's attention. "I'm supposed to love Theo Parker. A man, I should note, that currently wants nothing to do with me. And you're telling me that even after I make him fall for me, I'm not going to be able to be with him?"

Everybody zeroed in on Clementine, Parsnip, and Peach as they exchanged head tilts and nods as they casually agreed with each other as if the fate of their nieces wasn't in the balance.

"Yes, dear. We think that's right," Peach said after their brief contemplation. "Have you ever seen the movie *Practical Magic?*"

Alice pinched the space between her eyes. "Please tell me you're not referring to the *fictional* movie."

"Well, sure. They had to get their ideas from *somewhere*. It's basically just like that," Clementine said, all the while accepting overzealous agreement from her sisters. "Men hunted Bridget down."

"Oh, come on." Alice dropped her head while waiting for her aunts to pay yet another silent tribute to their beloved Bridget.

When Clementine finished, the bad news was confirmed. "So, in death, she cursed the women in our family. That we should never love a man."

Alice had no words, but she did grin a bit at the commentary coming from behind her.

"I've never wanted to be a lesbian so badly." The deadpan from Beatrice was appreciated. But it backfired.

Peach beamed. "There's the spirit! Take lemons and turn them into lemonade." Then Peach pinched her lips before wondering aloud. "Though, I'm not sure if the curse was about love in general, or if she just kind of blamed men for everything?"

"Helpful. *Very* helpful." Sarcasm dripped from every word. Alice followed it up with, "I'm going to need all the lemons I can get so I can turn them into a lemon martini."

"What a great idea!" Parsnip beamed. "I'll go get the lemons. You all just talk amongst yourselves while I'm gone."

Alice stole a look at her cousins, who were almost as mortified as she was.

Except for Riley. Riley seemed as if her newly discovered curse just lifted a weight off of her shoulders that she didn't even know was there.

I see you. Alice sent Riley the silent message. *And I'm going to discuss this with you the next time I get you alone.*

Riley shrugged and sent back, *What? I love the curse. It's going to make life far less complicated for me.*

Beck, ever the hopeful one, chimed in. "Hey, why can't we just find a way to reverse the curse? There's sure to be a way, right?"

Alice felt the hopeful energy from Beck and relished in the feeling for the first time since she walked into her version of *Halloween*. She was pretty sure not getting to love the man you knew you were *supposed* to love was the equivalent of getting slain by Michael Meyers. And at least in that scenario, he'd put her out of her misery.

"That's a great idea," Alice agreed, spinning in her circle of doom to look at Clementine and Peach, hopeful for a favorable response.

"They did it in *Practical Magic!*" Alice added a school-girl smile to show that she had been paying attention earlier *and* that she'd be willing to let her aunts pull the demons out – or whatever it was they did in that movie.

Upon entering the room with a tray full of lemon martinis, Parsnip laughed like Alice had nailed the punchline to the funniest joke in the world. "Oh, Alice. That's funny, dear. See, you're already trying to use your sense of humor. You'll forget about this guy and be your happy, normal self in no time."

Alice closed her mouth and turned around. She started to speak but just let her mouth hang open instead. It was no use. But to herself, she mumbled, "That wasn't a joke."

"Here's your drink, dear." Parsnip rolled forward and held out the tray of martinis.

"Now, on to more important things." Peach clapped happily before taking her own drink. "I know it's a bit of time away, but will you all be coming to the Winter Solstice?"

Alice took a big sip of her martini and asked the question for herself and her cousins behind her. "Will you be wearing clothes this time?"

CHAPTER 13

Theo spent the weekend outfitting his apartment. He got new sheets and a blanket for his bed. An alarm clock for his bedside table. And the biggest brand-new flat-screen TV he could find in town – which unfortunately topped out at a modest fifty-five inches. But he could suffer through a football game on fifty-five inches in a pinch.

And that's exactly how he spent his Sunday afternoon.

He'd gotten up early, taken a walk through town and down by the harbor. He picked up a black coffee at the diner where he'd met Franny, who, for running an easy-going Sunday morning kind of operation, wasn't as overly friendly as he expected she should be. At first, he wondered if he'd done something wrong, but Theo didn't think he'd been in town long enough to ruin anybody's day.

After that, he did a bit of wandering toward some of the farmland that sat on the edge of town, took in the morning fog that was just starting to burn off over the fields of pumpkins, corn stalks, and apple trees.

As the day crept closer to noon, Theo thought he'd try his luck once more at the diner to see if becoming a regular would change Franny's cold tune. He ordered a club sandwich at her recommendation and added a slice of pumpkin pie for good measure.

That time, she'd given him a reluctant nod which was better but still not great. But Theo must've done something right because he'd earned himself an extra side of French fries.

Sunday had been pretty close to the perfect day in his book. Theo wondered if he could go two-for-two.

While still lying in bed the following day, staring at the dark of his new ceiling, Theo's phone started to buzz.

"Hello?" Theo answered.

"Hey, I'm swinging by to pick you up. We're going to start a desensitization process."

Theo listened to Lane's chipper voice come through the receiver, loud and clear. And it sounded like he was already in his car.

"You're going to have to use smaller words this early in the morning. But, okay. When will you be here?" Theo asked.

"Two minutes."

Theo heard the click, gave himself another ten seconds of stillness, then left the warmth of the bed by whipping off the covers like he would rip off a Band-Aid – quickly to ease the pain of the cold fall weather.

Two minutes seemed enough time to get ready. Theo marched to the bathroom, brushed his teeth, washed his face, added a spritz of cologne since a shower seemed out of the question – though he'd thought about it for about a second – and dressed in his new uniform that he'd set out the night before. He buckled his belt, grabbed his hat, and just as he walked out the door, Lane pulled up alongside the curb.

"Morning," Theo said as he pulled himself into the cab of Lane's truck.

"Mornin' yourself." Lane grinned as he put the truck back into drive and rolled away into the stillness and quiet of the dark morning.

Theo couldn't help but wonder. "So, what's this I hear about a…de-sen–" He couldn't remember what Lane had said. There was no use in trying to sound out a word he couldn't recall.

"De-sens-it-iz-ation. Desensitization." When Lane said it the second time, it flowed out in a single fluid word, and his hand glided in front of him like it was something that just rolled off the tongue.

"Yeah, you're going to have to give me the Webster version of that one." Theo looked over and gave Lane a look that said he wasn't willing to try and put it together himself.

"We are going to get a coffee this morning – together." Lane nodded like the decision had been made.

Theo didn't think that sounded so bad. In fact, he loved coffee. "Sure, sounds great. I think I'm even starting to win Franny over – what with my double stop-in yesterday. Added a slice of the pumpkin pie." Theo was pretty keen on himself and his maneuvers into Franny's good graces.

"No. Not Franny's diner."

Theo blinked. He'd had his first night where he'd conjured up five glorious hours of sleep without Alice sneaking in. He wasn't going to give that up so easily.

"Nope. Not going in there."

"Yup. We're going in there."

"I slept well for the first time since driving into this crazy – yet, absolutely compelling town. I'm not giving that up so you can desensitize me to the bewitching good looks and strange charm of *that* woman." Theo thought about the words he'd just said. *Yup.* He wasn't going to back down.

"Here's my theory," Lane started.

"I'll hear it, but I'm not going to change my mind." Theo crossed his arms in defiance.

"I think you finally slept well *because* you interacted with Alice. I think the more you come to know her, the more…whatever it is that's got a grip on you will fade. She's a beautiful woman, no doubt. It's probably a shock to see and feel something for a creature like her after going through what you went through over the last year. Ease yourself in. Short trips. In-and-out for coffee. Pop in for an afternoon spice cookie or a pumpkin bar." Lane nodded to himself. "I think the more you see her, the less of an effect she'll have on you."

Theo sat with Lane's logic as they drove slowly through the town he'd all but thought of as his own in a matter of days. It wasn't a *completely* ridiculous notion. He supposed he could give it a try. Worst-case scenario, he'd be thinking about marriage again with a woman he'd said five words to, and he'd be right back where he was today. And if it didn't keep getting better, then he could just stop.

"Okay," Theo said after thinking it through. "I'll try for one week. But, if I start getting those crazy tornado, love-struck, marriage-like feelings again, I'm stopping her cold turkey."

Lane beamed. "Works for me!"

Within five minutes, the two men were hovering near the outside of the coffee shop. Theo's hands were clammy, and Lane was enjoying his discomfort entirely too much.

"This *process* is a terrible idea." Theo could already feel his heart pounding.

What in the heck was that? Was he having an anxiety attack over a woman he really didn't even know?

"You'll be fine. What's the worst that can happen?" Lane asked while putting a less-than-comforting hand on Theo's shoulder.

"Ah, I propose marriage to a woman I've said five words to? That seems pretty bad." Theo stared at the door, nervous, like a man who *was* actually preparing to ask for a woman's hand.

"Come on. Buck up. In, order coffee, small talk, out. Quick and efficient." Lane chopped his hand through the air, making a point for every step listed.

Theo inhaled deeply and blew it out through puffy cheeks. He shook his head, bounced a couple times like a football player preparing to return a kickoff, and lightly slapped the sides of his face for good measure.

"Okay," Theo finally said. "Let's do this."

Lane opened the door, and Theo stood in place. Lane chuckled and shook his head. Then, to offer a little encouragement, he said, "After you, buddy."

Theo looked at Lane like he didn't realize it was his turn to walk in. "Right." He shook his head and hands, sucked in a breath, then took a step inside.

Immediately he felt like he'd been lassoed. Theo looked in the direction of the pull.

There she was. Freaking glowing. Her feet barely skimming the ground as she laughed like she'd just heard her customer tell her the funniest thing in the world.

"I can't do it." Theo started to turn, only this time, Lane didn't have to stop him. Whatever invisible rope that had been strung around him was holding him in place.

Lane gave Theo a sideways glance when he watched as Theo looked like he tried to walk out but that his feet were glued to the ground. "Sure, you can. Looks to me like your subconscious knows better and wants you to stay. Now, let's go. Just a couple more feet."

It was like trying to move a stubborn donkey.

Then the worst thing happened. Well, Grumbles letting out a long, low bark and thumping his tail on the floor, wasn't actually so bad. But the moment Alice looked up at the commotion *was* the worst.

He felt like a teenager. In the thick of awkward adolescence, about to go on his first date. Or, like he was about to make an attempt at kissing the high school girl of his dreams.

He'd experienced something similar in high school. He'd dreamed of his young crush, Stacey Carlson, every night, too. But, this was different. This was *definitely* different.

"She's the worst." Theo didn't realize he'd said the words out loud – or that those were the particular words that made it out. Because inside his head, the whole thing went something like: *She's the worst…because I have a feeling this is going to cause me a lot more trouble than it already is.*

Lane pulled Theo forward with his hand on a stiff arm. "She's not the worst. You've never even had a civilized conversation with her."

"Because I don't want to," Theo admitted.

Lane ignored the rebuttal. "Do you want to know who *is* actually the worst?"

"Yes."

"Trish." Lane stopped and looked Theo dead in the eye. "I need you to listen to me right now. Trish is the worst. What you need, my friend is…a friend. A *female* friend. So, snap out of this funk, quit feeling sorry for yourself and acting like you just saw a ghost, and go up and talk to Alice. She's as innocent as they come. Hasn't ever even had a boyfriend. How harmful can she *really* be?"

Theo looked over at Alice, who was looking magnificent, while waving at him. He lifted a hand in response, then let it fall.

Harmless my rear-end.

But, Theo did suppose if he didn't act on any of his psychotic feelings – like love and marriage – maybe he could start a *very* short conversation. *Maybe.*

Lane had efficiently – if agonizingly slowly – moved Theo to a position just on the other side of the register.

"Hey, guys!" Alice beamed, and Theo felt the bolt of lightning to his heart. "I'm so glad you stopped by. What can I get you?"

Lane elbowed Theo in the arm.

"Uh, hi." Theo cleared his throat. "Latte. Sweet. Big one."

He lingered like he was going to say more. And usually, he would have been put together enough to notice the amused way Alice was pinching her lips together. But, unfortunately, due to the battle going on between his head and his heart, he wasn't all there. So, all he said was, "And, thank you."

"Of course. One large sweetened latte coming right up. Want any extra additions?"

Theo watched Alice nod her head toward the board that hung above them that offered things like *destressing, energy, confidence* – which Theo thought was interesting. Had he been able to laugh at the situation and his mediocre self-control, he would have suggested that she add them all just to get a good laugh.

"No." It was all he could muster.

Man, Theo told himself, *Trish really messed with your mind.*

"Lane? How about you?" Alice gave Lane the same happy smile.

"I'll take the usual with a boost of energy. I'm feeling a good day coming on," Lane admitted.

"You got it. And, I like it!"

As Alice was steaming milk and brewing the espresso, Paige walked in while finishing the double-knot on her apron.

"Morning!" Paige said, sounding exactly like Alice. "Can I take over for you?" she asked Alice, who was adding pumps of maple syrup to Lane's cup.

"That'd be great, Paige," Alice started, getting the young woman's attention. "Have you officially met Theo Parker? He's our new deputy."

Paige's eyes grew wide with realization. And all Alice could do was smile and nod – not needing to read the young woman's mind to know inside she was screaming, *Oh my gosh! That's* your *Theo Parker!*

But, Alice did read Paige's mind because her thoughts were screaming so loudly it was almost impossible not to. And they were giving Theo a ten in all categories – especially the looks department.

"Nice to meet you, Mr. Parker." The devilish way Paige said the words had Alice choking back a laugh.

Theo kept his eyes on Alice most of the time. Except when he had to shift them occasionally to acknowledge Paige.

He even considered it progress that he was able to answer Alice's next question.

"How was your first weekend in town, Theo?" Alice rested a hip on the counter and looked at him as if he was the only man in the universe.

"Ah, um. Good. Yeah," Theo said, agreeing with himself. "Good. Walks, diner. Football."

Lane gave Theo a reassuring slap on the back. A one-handed *you're doing great, man. Now, reciprocate.*

"You? I mean, yours?" Theo managed to stammer out the question.

Theo watched Alice's eyes turn an impossible shade of ice blue as she lost herself in thought. It seemed otherworldly, and it sucked him in. Even Grumbles let out a low ruff. It made him want to ask if she was okay. He could have sworn he saw a flicker of disappointment before smiling again and saying, "It was lovely. I was able to share an evening with my aunts and all of my cousins. I'll remember the moments forever."

Theo wasn't entirely sure if Alice was pleased about that. But he'd done his job, and that was enough. He didn't need to learn anything further about her. At least for now. He was okay with the tiniest baby step that would allow him to survive.

Paige handed Lane his latte, intentionally leaving Theo's for Alice to handle. And all the progress Theo thought he'd made in those brief minutes was gone the minute their fingers touched.

Suddenly, Theo imagined his fingers running through Alice's curls and cupping her face to bring her into a long, tender kiss.

Theo yanked his hand away, splashing a bit of the latte on his new uniform. But that was the least of his worries. He was not ready to be infatuated with this woman – this nice woman.

Keeping his head down, Theo marched out the door, leaving Lane, Paige, and Alice staring after him.

When the door swung open again, they all jumped at the surprise of it. Once more, they were all looking at Theo.

"Just so we're clear. I *will* come here because you give me delicious coffee and exchange in very – and I mean *very* – casual conversation. It will *not* be because you are beautiful, funny, clever, or nice…or any of the really great things people say about you. Though, I do think under normal – not these – circumstances, all of those are fortunate qualities to have." Theo turned again. And stopped again. Then said, "Good day." And marched out of the door for a second time.

"He's *the* Theo Parker!" Paige exclaimed as if she hadn't just witnessed one of the strangest goodbyes. "He really is so handsome. I hadn't noticed when he tripped out of the shop the first time, but can I just say – *wow*."

Paige rambled on while Alice and Lane exchanged humored looks for two very different reasons.

"He just *good day'd* me," Alice said, finally.

"Yes. Yes, he did," Lane agreed, not knowing how else to comment on his friend's behavior.

"We're making great progress!" Alice was more than satisfied with the exchange.

Curse-smurse. They'd be sharing more than minute-long exchanges in no time.

CHAPTER 14

"I think I figured it out," Willa grunted while hoisting another pumpkin onto the old wooden flat-bed truck – her favorite farm vehicle.

Alice and Riley both held their breath as they cradled a gigantic pumpkin between the both of them, waddling toward the same truck. They set it down with a thud.

"Oh, for goodness sake. This is just…hocus pocus."

Riley grinned at Alice's choice of words. But was thankful for her resignation.

Alice let herself fall to the ground. Then, with a bit of concentration and without touching the pumpkin, she used her hands – palms up – to lift it onto the truck.

"Okay." Alice stretched out in the open field, then rolled to her side to give Willa her attention. "What do you have figured out?"

Willa hopped up on the edge of the truck bed and leaned forward. "I scoured every book I had on curses. And I think I know how to break it. Or, I should say, how Theo can break it."

Alice pushed up and knelt, now very interested. If it meant breaking the curse, she was all in. She walked on her knees until her hands gripped Willa's. "What do you mean *Theo can break it?*"

"From what I gather, he either has to willingly fall in love with you, or he has to be your soulmate. I'm a little fuzzy on the details." Willa shrugged.

Alice sat back. "What do you mean *fuzzy on the details?* Those are two very different things. It's like–" Alice searched for an example. "Like, comparing passionate attraction and the disembodied spirit of a dead person." Alice's head traveled from Willa to Riley and back again. "So, I either need to sleep with him or kill him?"

Riley let her laugh slip, earning a quick shock from Alice and her narrowed eyes.

"Ow! Hey." Riley rubbed her hand where she felt the spark. "I'm laughing because it's astounding to me what you learned from your lessons. Or, I should say, what you *didn't* learn."

"Well…" Alice huffed, looking for a way to defend herself. When she came up one thought short of a full spellbook, she gave in. "Then humor me."

This time Riley smiled. "What I'm sure Willa knows as well is: the term *soul mate* originated in the early eighteen-hundreds."

Willa nodded, letting Riley know she should keep moving since she was moving in the right direction.

"And yes, one meaning could result in Theo's death. But the other could mean that in this scenario, your souls are connected in your thoughts, actions, and feelings. Everything right down to your moral compass. Basically, your entire spiritual being is connected to him." Riley finished and waited.

Alice sat on her heels, letting the words sink in.

Willa decided to offer encouragement. "I think the latter explains all of the ethereal, earth-shifting moments you and Theo have shared. And he *does* feel them. Everything you feel – Theo feels. Except you know magic, and he doesn't. I'm surprised he even looks at you after all the crazy things you've put him through."

"It's not like I'm trying," Alice defended herself. "It just happens."

There was another moment of silence as the autumn wind whipped around them. Then Alice asked, "So, this is actually a good thing?"

Willa shrugged and gave a half-hearted nod.

"What? What is…that?" Alice exaggerated her mimic of Willa's actions. "I've never seen anything more noncommittal in my life."

Willa started slowly. "I just think…that…well, I guess, I just don't know what happens if he decides to not love you back. That's where I'm foggy. It could be that I'm unable to pinpoint it because I'm cursed, too."

"It wouldn't be a very good curse if we knew how to break it." Riley fell to the ground and rested her head on Alice's legs.

Alice looked down. "You're not helping."

"Hey, I helped with the soulmate part."

Alice moved a brown strand of hair from Riley's face. "It was greatly appreciated." Then she gave her cheek a friendly tap. "But now, I need to know what I can do to make sure my handsome soulmate decides to love me." Alice slumped. "Because it's not really a secret that he's pretty hell-bent on avoiding me."

When neither of her cousins took the bait, Alice argued for herself. "Oh, come on," she pleaded. "We are making progress!"

"Alice." Riley tilted her head back. "The poor guy can barely look you in the eyes. He stumbles over words like you stumble over your spellbooks."

"Not nice."

Riley grinned.

"I think what Riley is trying to say," Willa interjected, "is he's going to need a little help. Or, some therapy." Now it was Willa's turn to smile.

"You're both *hilarious.*"

"He just needs a little nudge," Willa said finally as she jumped off the bed of the truck.

With a quick look around to make sure nobody was watching, Willa raised both arms and lifted all of the pumpkins from that section of the field and floated them over to the truck. She loved farming, but they had a Fall Festival to set up for. Besides, a little magic in the name of efficiency never hurt.

CHAPTER 15

Theo was pacing back and forth in his new – well, actually ancient – office building when Beck walked in with lunch.

The town of Lantern Lane did things like that: ordered lunch from a diner in the middle of the day, then stopped to enjoy it with coworkers or friends.

The small town was also decidedly less criminal than the city he came from. As a result, it left more time for *getting to know* his neighbors, assisting in street cleanup, helping set up for the Fall Festival, and ensuring the celebration went off without a hitch. He actually helped an older woman carry her groceries across the street earlier that day. And, as Theo was experiencing now, it left him way too much time to think.

"You're looking…contemplative?" Beck tried to nail down just what Theo was feeling, but with the way his mind was zigzagging all over the place, she couldn't find a better word.

Beck motioned for Theo to join her at their long conference table that sat right out in the open in the front room and yelled back to Lane to let him know lunch had arrived.

Theo rubbed his hands down the sleep-deprived, stubble-filled creases on his face, and he looked hopelessly at Beck.

"Beck." Theo started. "Let's just say you had strong feelings for…*somebody*. Somebody you barely knew. You'd just gotten out of a terrible relationship–"

"Over a year ago." Lane smiled as he added what he felt was a necessary detail to Theo's soon to be question.

"Right. But she *was* awful." Theo earned a nod from Lane. "So, the idea of jumping right back into all that *feeling* again seems…terrifying."

"I think the idea of love is terrifying," Beck said, without having been asked a question.

"And you'd avoid it?" *Naturally.* Theo thought he was about to be reassured.

"Absolutely not."

"What?"

"Of course not. The things that are most terrifying are the most worth it." Beck shrugged and took a huge bite of her deli-style sandwich. Then followed it up with an eye-watering glug of root beer. She lifted her eyebrows at the appreciation on Lane's face.

"So, what you're saying is: I just need to accept that I'm hallucinating, not sleeping, dreaming so vividly it's basically like not sleeping, living through tornadoes caused by a woman's touch, and just get to know Alice?" Theo stared across the table at Beck.

She smiled and said, "Yup."

When Theo dropped his forehead to the wooden tabletop, Lane laughed. Lane assumed everything Theo just listed off was a figment of his imagination or a dramatization of events to prove how miserable he was. Then Lane looked at Beck and said, "Dude's got it bad."

Beck nodded, then agreed aloud. "You have *no* idea."

CHAPTER 16

It was the first rainy day Lantern Lane had seen since their summer turned into an early fall. The gray sky cast a moody hue over the browns, reds, and yellows of the season. And the sidewalks and streets glistened with dampness while the streetlamps blurred through the thick drops.

Alice didn't mind the rain. In fact, when she was contemplating a new potion, she preferred it.

Turning away from her second-floor window, Alice crossed her arms as she stared at her cauldron that sat across the room. She lifted a brow, wondering if she was heading down a path of questionable ethics. Historically, witches didn't really pay much attention to whether or not what they were doing was right or wrong – it just kind of *was*.

But this? Alice asked herself as she lifted one of her crossed arms to tap a finger on her chin to help her deliberate.

"Hmm, what do you think?" Alice asked Grumbles, who was enjoying the rainy day for an entirely different reason. He was using it as an excuse to stretch his enormous brown body over his dog bed that took up about half of the living room.

Grumbles didn't bother moving his body; he just rolled his head and let his ears flop backward, and his lips and cheeks sag from the gravity.

When he didn't say anything, Alice tried again. "Well?"

This time, Grumbles groaned, gave a little shake of his head, then dropped it back into place, half on and half off of the bed.

"Yeah," Alice said quietly, still eyeing the big black iron pot. "You're probably right."

She didn't break her gaze when her phone rang; she simply lifted it to her ear and said, "Hi."

"Tell me what you're doing right now." Riley didn't have to be in the room to know Alice's tone meant she was up to no good.

"I'm not doing anything," Alice said, trying to sound as casual as possible.

"It's not a good idea."

"You don't even know what I'm thinking about." Alice inched closer to the cauldron.

"I don't have to. I can feel your conflict from here. I'm just telling you that whatever you're thinking about doing: it's not a good idea. Remember, you can't use magic on Theo. It's part of the curse."

"Well, not directly. *But* if he happens to drink a beverage as a result of his *own free will*, that's technically not *me* using magic on him, is it?"

Alice smirked victoriously as the words spilled out. She'd worked hard to come to that rationalization the night before. She'd spent hours wracking her brain thinking of some way to give Theo that *nudge* that Willa had mentioned in the pumpkin patch.

Alice mindlessly started pulling vials out of her cabinet and placing them on her table. She thought Riley wouldn't be able to put the sporadic movements together if she mindlessly went through the motions.

It didn't work.

"No," Riley said through the other end. "Stop right now. I'm coming over." There was a short pause before Riley spoke again. "Do I need everybody?"

"No! And…no."

Alice realized her stand-off was no longer with the giant vessel.

She and Riley stood, unmoving, with their phones to their ears – a silent dare from one witch to another. Riley daring Alice to stop. And Alice daring Riley to try and stop her.

After ten long seconds, there were no goodbyes. Just a rush to their own respective victory.

Alice tried to feel Riley's progress across town. While she did, she frantically poured liquids, spices, fresh herbs, a few items that would probably disgust the average human into the cauldron. Then, with a snap of her fingers, a blazing fire roared to life. All she needed now was a boil. Just a hint of a boil.

Alice drummed her fingers on her hips as she looked from the potion to the door, willing the mix to boil.

"Why is it that we can do almost *everything* with magic, but we can't make something boil faster?" Alice asked Grumbles, who had taken an interest in the flame. He ignored the question but rolled his body over so he was closer to the heat.

Alice narrowed her eyes at his new, warmer position. "I'll remember this moment the next time you're trying to get your soulmate to fall in love with you."

Then she saw it: the first bubble.

She dipped, so her eyes became level with the liquid and watched as two more bubbles made that beautiful, distinctive thick *plop*. Her eyes widened with greed, and she knew there was only one more step.

Alice reached for the clip she'd used to cinch her hair back that morning, and just as her red waves fell around her face, Riley threw open the door.

"Don't. Even. Think about it." Riley pointed her finger at Alice, who was now holding a single, long curl that was still connected to her head.

Alice yanked.

"No!" Riley yelled.

Alice moved her eyes from the cauldron to Riley. "Why not?"

"You can't give your soulmate a love potion." Riley took a step forward but stopped when Alice threatened to drop the strand.

Alice blinked. "*Why* not?"

Riley opened her mouth to speak. Then she closed it.

Riley's face softened as she lowered her hands and said, "I…I don't know?"

Alice's lips turned up in a helpless grin. She shrugged, showing she didn't know what else to do. "I have to do something."

Riley walked up to Alice and stood next to her, peering into the boiling concoction. "Maybe it's because I don't understand." Riley looked at Alice, waiting for an explanation.

Shrugging again, Alice shook her head. "It's like…I know with every fiber of my being that he's the person for me. He's the solidarity to my discord. Though," Alice thought aloud, "I'm not certain he isn't also the one causing my discord. I've never felt the need to love a man before. And now, it's like I'll go crazy if I can't."

Alice took a breath and put a hand on Riley's arm. "I *have* to do something."

Riley mirrored Alice's long breath, then nodded. "If this goes terribly wrong, we'll just blame Willa."

Alice beamed. "Works for me!"

Then she dropped the red strand of hair into the love potion.

CHAPTER 17

The first day of the Fall Festival had finally arrived, and with it, the perfect autumn day. The sun was shining and warm, and the breeze was cool and crisp.

Alice had opened Witches' Brew for the early morning rush and was greeted by an excited crowd of townspeople and visitors from around the area.

The Fall Festival was when Lantern Lane was at its best. The town – and the witches who lived there – made sure of that. Alice, who was both of those things, was a large part of the perfection.

Alice began shutting the coffee shop down an hour before she was due at her festival coffee stand. This year she had a prime location right next to Franny's diner pastries and hand pies. What went better together than a delicious snack and a warm seasonal – slightly magical – drink?

After ten minutes of cleanup and fifty minutes of staring at the tiny vial she'd created just the day before, Alice's conscience was getting the better of her. Unfortunately, there wasn't any amount of pacing - with or without Grumbles by her side - that had proved helpful. And every time she went to pick up the vial, Grumbles lifted his head, and well…grumbled.

"Hey!" Paige bounded into the back room just in time to see Alice pull her hand away from the vial on the counter, jumping backward about three feet.

"Whoa, sorry," Paige said, laughing. "Hey, big guy." Paige made sure to bend over and scratch Grumbles' ears.

Alice laughed at the humor of the moment while she placed a calming hand on her chest. "Paige, oh my gosh, sorry. I thought I was alone. Are we all set?"

"We are. Everything is ready except for this last batch of apple cider. I thought I could bring it over for you?" Paige made the offer with a devious smile.

Alice narrowed her knowing eyes at the energetic employee and grinned. "Who is he?"

"How did you know?" Paige asked, astonished – not knowing that Alice had literally seen right through her.

"You're glowing. Is *he* coming to the festival today?"

"*He* is Patrick, and yes, he's there already! I saw him through the street barriers at the edge of the Lane with a bunch of his friends. I thought maybe I could have our booth set up by the time he got there."

Alice softened. "You're the most wonderful young woman in the world." Her hand found Paige's cheek, and her young friend blushed. "Go crazy," Alice said, finally.

Alice and Paige looked to the door when the bell hanging above it chimed.

"Alice, you here?"

Alice knew Riley had walked through the door before she heard her voice. "We're back here!"

"Hey." Riley walked in sporting a ridiculous neon orange t-shirt with giant printed letters scrawled across the front, boasting that *BOOKS SAVE LIVES*.

Alice looked her up and down, then tilted her head a bit, questioning the choice in fashion.

Riley answered the look. "Hey, I make reading look good. Just you wait and see how all the children flock to me."

Alice and Paige exchanged grins. "I like your enthusiasm. But I would probably choose a better way to say that. *Hocus Pocus* kind of gave a bad name to the whole *wanting children to flock to you* thing."

Riley considered the suggestion. "Noted." Then she smiled. "Can I think about it while you help me bring all of the super cool children's books to my stand at the festival?"

Alice looked at Paige. "You got this?"

"Absolutely! Go."

Alice squeezed Paige's hand, then followed Riley through the coffee shop and out the front door with Grumbles trotting at their heels.

Before Paige loaded the work cart with the two remaining jugs of apple cider, she spotted the small vial on the counter. Since it looked like all of the others that Alice had instructed her to add to various Witches' Brew drinks, she picked it up, dropped it into her pocket, and started pushing the cart toward the exit.

"Well, what did you decide?" Riley asked as they walked into Riley's book store and grabbed the final boxes of books that would be on display and for sale at the festival.

Alice shrugged. "I don't know if it's the guilt, my conscience getting the best of me, the curse starting to scare me a little, or Grumbles starting to infiltrate my mind."

"You're not going to use the potion?" Riley asked, pausing before she pushed the door open to the sidewalk.

"No." Alice shook her head. "I'm not. It's not fair to Theo. I feel like I need him to love me, but that's not a reason to force those kinds of feelings on him."

"That's very…*human* of you." Riley nudged Alice with the side of her arm, then turned to Grumbles. "Good dog!"

"I'm not sure if I should take that as a compliment," Alice admitted while she watched Riley give her giant brown dog credit for her good decision-making.

"It's one of the best qualities you have as a witch. Ready?" Riley nodded toward the door, asking if Alice was ready to step out into the festival.

"Ready."

The street was already bustling with people in flannel shirts, sweaters, and vests. Some were stopping at vendors who were selling everything from painted pumpkins to festive broomsticks. Others were taking crisp, chewy bites of sticky, sweet caramel apples on pointy sticks and deep-fried slices of pumpkin pie.

Alice smiled at the happiness and wonder she saw in everybody. She could *feel* the elation in the kids running through the crowds, tugging their parents behind them. And she reveled in the satisfaction and joy emanating from every being that was old enough to appreciate the small, beautiful moments of life.

"It's my favorite time of the year, too." Riley stood next to Alice, rested her head on Alice's shoulder, and agreed with Alice's thoughts while Grumbles leaned into Alice from the other side.

Alice and Riley stood for a moment as they let the happiness from the townspeople pour through them.

Then, when Grumbles lifted his head from resting on Alice's hip, his ears perked into an alert position, and a small wine whimpered through his furry lips.

That's when everything started to go wrong.

CHAPTER 18

Their thoughts were still happy when Alice and Riley lifted their heads in concern. They tried to focus on where the chaos was coming from, then they both turned their heads toward the Witches' Brew festival stand at the same time.

"You didn't," Riley said.

"No!" Alice shook her head and looked back to Riley and repeated, "No. I told you I didn't."

Their eyes grew wide. Then at the same time, they said, "Paige!"

Riley and Alice hurried to the book booth and dropped the boxes. Then they stood and stared at each other while the frantic thoughts from a few townspeople started rolling in.

Where's Alice? I need to confess my love.

Alice is my everything, my world. I love her.

What I would give to see Alice nak–

"It's getting worse!" Alice yelled the statement so she wouldn't hear the last thought as it echoed from the people around her.

The gurgle of laughter from Riley sputtered out before either of them was ready for it. Alice's eyes went wide with shock at the unexpected thought.

Embarrassed, Alice swatted at Riley's arm. "Hey! That's not funny. That's…*disturbing.*"

Riley could barely contain herself. "Mr. Swenson! Who knew?"

"Riley. No more." Alice looked mortified. "Mr. Swenson is at least one hundred years old."

"At *least.* But he's still got a good appetite for your apple cider…and your…*apples!*" Riley billowed over in a roar of laughter.

"You're having way too much fun with this," Alice whispered as she looked around, hoping nobody could hear them. "We have to get that cider out of the booth. *Now.*"

"Alice! Oh, Alice!"

Alice gently punched a hunched over Riley multiple times to get her attention before turning around to see a roly-poly Mrs. Hendricks. Mrs. Hendricks was happily married to her husband, Mr. Gary Hendricks, and had just celebrated their forty-second anniversary.

"Mrs. Hendricks. It's so nice to see you. How are you today?" Alice asked, trying to sound like she would have any other day of the week.

Mrs. Hendricks looked like her eyeballs turned into hearts. And she ignored the question. "Have I ever told you how much I adore–"

"My apple cider?" Alice almost screamed out the interruption. She couldn't let Mrs. Hendricks say what was on her mind.

Riley gave another snorting laugh and sent a thought to Alice, *Mrs. Hendricks is an animal!*

"Oh," Mrs. Hendricks swooned. "Your apple cider is just so wonderful. But Alice, so are you."

Alice spat out a new mouthful of words while grabbing Riley's hand and tugging her out of the booth. "Okay. Thank you, Mrs. Hendricks. Tell Mr. Hendricks – *your husband* – hello for me."

Alice sprinted for cover behind a large booth filled with fat pumpkins and gourds. Barely allowing Riley to keep up, Alice crouched and maneuvered like an undercover operative.

Grumbles didn't seem to care about getting caught. Instead, he took his time trotting behind them and plopped his butt on the ground.

Alice gave him a slanty eye and said, "A little quicker, Buster." Then she scratched his forehead fondly before darting her eyes back to her stand.

"I *need* to tell the cousins," Riley said through her hysterics. "They are going to think this is hilarious."

"Riley!" Alice looked shocked.

"I mean, they might be able to help."

Alice squinted at the woman who claimed to be her best friend but who was acting more like an annoying little cousin at the moment.

Deciding to avoid the topic for the more pressing matter at hand, Alice ignored Riley's comment. Then she started her instruction.

"Here's what we're going to do." Alice lowered her eyes to make sure Riley was paying attention. "You're going to run over and tell Paige to help you take the apple cider containers back to the shop. Then, I'll go around back and meet you over there. And *you*." Alice pointed at Grumbles. "You are on overly affectionate people duty. If *anybody* is extra nice to me, you cause a scene. Do you understand?"

Grumbles barked in response.

"Good boy."

"Wait," Riley said. "Around back? How come you're not coming to help?"

"Uh, hello? Can you not hear the thoughts coming from all of those people? Did you *see* and *hear* Mrs. Hendricks?"

"I did. And, can I just say, you made a *fabulous* love potion." Riley nodded, trying to hold in her smile and a new round of laughter. "The aunts would be *very* proud."

"That isn't funny."

"Okay." Riley covered her pinched smile. "I'll do it."

Alice softened and exhaled a sigh of relief. "Thank you."

"Hey."

When Alice and Riley heard the voice coming from above them, they slowly turned their heads up together.

Alice's heart raced at the sight of him, then plummeted at the unmistakable white paper cup in his hand.

"Hey," Alice said to an unbelievably handsome Theo Parker.

Riley shot up, startling Alice and Theo. "Well, ah, I gotta run. Talk later. Nice seeing you, Theo."

Alice swiped at Riley's shirt to get her to stay but instead missed and landed on all-fours.

Theo raised a hand and said, "Ah, yeah. You, too." But Riley was already halfway to the cider bins, approaching a peppy Paige who was doling out drink cups like her life depended on it.

When Theo looked down and held out a hand to help Alice from her crouched position, Alice couldn't believe it. Theo was suddenly willing to touch her? She shouldn't do it.

She shouldn't take his hand. Not this way. But what would happen? Alice was too curious to know.

She eyed the cup in Theo's hand. Looked at how it was cradled next to his body. Then the other hand that was still extended out to her.

She reached up, then hesitated a moment.

But on cue, Grumbles started howling. Then, as commanded, he began rolling around on the ground and barking like a lunatic in between them both.

"Wait! No, Grumbles!" Alice lurched forward, tackling the dog that doubled her in size. She wrapped her hands around his nose like she had many times before when they were playing, only this time, she was also begging him *not* to cause a scene.

Grumbles froze with his paws in the air, staring at his owner, giving her a look that said, *I'm just doing what you told me to do.*

"I know. Good dog." Alice scratched his belly when she pushed back to her knees. "You did really great."

Alice heard the thoughts before she saw that Grumbles' commotion had given her away.

She looked up at Theo and saw a man who looked like he was staring at the craziest exchange he'd ever seen between a woman and her dog. *But* his hand was still outstretched.

Theo had avoided her, avoided his feelings – *their* feelings. And now, after a single cup, he was still extending his hand to her. A willing touch – even after she'd just publicly wrestled with her dog.

Alice tentatively lifted her hand once more and watched as Theo moved it the rest of the way to grip her hand.

As he pulled her up, their earth shook. He closed his eyes for a brief second as if he was making sure the feeling was real. Then he opened them again and found Alice staring directly at him.

When their hands parted, everything stilled.

Alice wished she knew what he was thinking. He still seemed nervous, but he was still there. And he wasn't running in the other direction. Instead, he was looking right at her.

Progress!

But as much as Alice wanted to savor the moment, she saw both Riley and Paige carry the cider dispensers away, *and* two other townspeople lock eyes with her. One she knew, and the other she'd never seen in her life. And both were sending her *hey baby* vibes.

"Okay. Okay," Alice said, then looked at Theo. "Want to get out of here?" Alice asked, knowing she absolutely sounded like she was nuts. But really, didn't he already think she was?

"Ah." Theo looked around, confused. Then back to Alice. "Sure?"

Alice ignored his noncommittal, question-like response. "Great!"

She grabbed his hand again and dragged him toward the book store.

As they ran, they navigated the earthquake their touch created. But even with all of the commotion and uncertainty, Alice knew she had never felt more alive or wonderful.

CHAPTER 19

The last row of bookshelves, in the back of the bookstore, was where Alice had led Theo. She didn't realize she'd be hunched over next to him, hiding from an unknown number of people, while staring at the long-haired Amazonian-looking men on the book covers in the romance novel section. But she had to admit, the time alongside Theo was nice.

Alice struggled to breathe from their quick escape as she stared forward to get the chaos of her thoughts straight. But, when Grumbles trotted around the corner and sat next to them in the back row, she couldn't help but smile when Theo scratched his head.

She couldn't see inside of him, read his thoughts, or use magic on him like she could with anybody else, but in her heart, she knew he was a good man.

Sporting a cute yet still tentative grin, Theo squatted next to Alice. "So, are you okay?"

Alice's eyebrows shot up. "Yes, of course. Why?"

"Ah." Theo looked around. "Just, the whole..." Theo didn't quite know how to explain it. So instead, he asked, "Are you hiding?"

"Oh." Alice panicked just a little. "No, no. I was just checking in on Paige. You know, making sure she's toeing the line, see who she's giving drinks to...the usual." Alice could feel Grumbles roll his eyes. "But, then you were there, I didn't want to get caught, and I thought how nice it would be for us to be able to have a pleasant conversation without all of the chaos from the festival."

Theo stared, then nodded.

"How do you like it? In Lantern Lane, I mean." Alice worked quickly to change the topic, and she rejoiced when she saw Theo physically relax.

"I love it. Which is saying something," Theo admitted while he rested his head on a shirtless man on a book behind him. "I had every intention of leaving after I chipped in on the force for a bit and got some time away. Maybe a couple months, maybe a year, then head out. But, I have to admit, I'm drawn to it. I don't know if I could leave even if I tried."

Theo meant it. Even with all of the weird stuff that he'd been experiencing in Lantern Lane, he *literally* didn't think he'd be able to leave. Like some crazy, cosmic force was keeping him here.

And strangely enough, almost all of the wacky things seemed to involve Alice. Whether it was in person, in his dreams, or the reminders of her that he constantly saw throughout the day.

The weirdest part of it all – even with all the crazy, strange things – he didn't *want* to leave.

Alice watched Theo's face as his mind worked out the details of what he'd just said and couldn't help the grin that found her face.

"Well," she said, finally, "I'd like it if you stayed."

Their eyes held for a second too long, and Theo looked away. He needed baby steps. After all, this was the first day of acting on his insane impulses. He should take it slow.

Seeing the hesitation, Alice rushed to think of something that wouldn't have Theo running away from her again. But before she realized what she was saying, Alice spewed out the words in her mind. "Why are you so scared of me?!"

What the…

Alice wanted to smack herself in the head. Of *all* of the things she could have said, asked, or experienced in awkward silence, *that* is what she went with?

She'd like to sandwich her head between a spellbook and hide for the foreseeable future. Or, at least until Theo took the chance to run as far away from her as possible. And she actually paused to give him the opportunity to do just that. In fact, after a question like that, she wouldn't blame him.

When Theo didn't run – or clumsily fall as he staggered away from her in the opposite direction – Alice felt a small, newt-sized nugget of hope spark inside of her.

Theo laughed self-consciously. How exactly did you tell a woman you've known for mere minutes combined over a matter of days that you're infatuated with her. *Without* sounding like a lunatic? That last part was key.

He wasn't one to lie. And he was done running from her. Or, at least he'd give it his best shot. So, a partial truth would have to do for today. And a partial truth wouldn't be denying that he wasn't terrified, *but* he also didn't have to come right out and say that either.

"You're beautiful. Like, too beautiful."

That was it? Alice blinked, and Grumbles covered his face with his paws.

When he realized even Grumbles was disappointed in him, embarrassed for him, or taking pity on him, Theo knew he had to elaborate.

"Bad relationship. She was...pretty." Theo stole a quick look at Alice. "But not like you. Pretty enough," he settled on. "It didn't end well. She, uh, decided to have two relationships outside of ours. It might be old-fashioned, but I'm a one-woman kind of guy. Anyway, she blindsided me. Embarrassed me. And, I suppose, ruined me a bit."

Alice's heart broke for Theo and what he'd gone through. She decidedly did *not* like whomever it was that he was in that relationship with. But she didn't understand what that had to do with her being beautiful. And the truth was, she couldn't really relate to either side.

She shrugged. "I've never been in a relationship."

Theo couldn't believe it. How could a woman like Alice not be at the top of the list for every eligible bachelor? But, he did have to admit, it made her seem a little less intimidating.

Maybe he could let himself get to know Alice. It's not like he needed to act impulsively by pulling her in and kissing her like crazy. Or by wrapping his fingers in her unruly red curls. Or by pulling her into his body for a long, intimate embrace.

No. Theo didn't have to do any of that – because *that's* what terrified him.

What he *could* do was start slowly. Have friendly conversations with her. Get to know her over coffees, lunches at the diner...for as long as they both shall live.

"No!" Theo said aloud, adamantly disagreeing with dangerous thoughts plaguing his mind.

"Sorry?" Alice asked, wondering if she should be ashamed she'd never wanted a relationship – until Theo.

Alice tried hard to concentrate on Theo. On what he was about to say, his mannerisms, his handsome facial features, but she couldn't. The thoughts of all of those apple cider-drinking love-struck mortals were crashing her mind.

"No, no. Sorry. Not you," Theo said. How was it possible he'd become so uncool, so quickly? "I would like to get to know you."

The surprise showed on Alice's face; her wide eyes accompanied an excited grin.

Isn't Alice the cat's meow?

Where is Alice Balfour?

I wonder if Alice would like to take a ride through the hayfields with me?

The bell above Riley's book shop door chimed, forcing Alice to shut off the voices. She had to get out of there. She needed to take cover, or she was going to scare Theo into changing his mind. Besides, she was pretty sure she heard Theo said he wanted to get to know her through the jumble of thoughts pouring in.

"Alice?" The question came from a voice wandering through the book stacks. "Alice, are you in here?"

"Theo," Alice whispered, "I think getting to know you sounds like the best thing I've ever heard." She crawled to the edge of the bookcase they were hiding behind and peeked around the edge before looking back. "How do you feel about pumpkins?"

When Theo pointed toward the sound, wondering if Alice wanted to stand and perhaps talk with the person looking for her, she shook her head so quickly Theo thought it might fall off. But the action had done its job in stopping him from standing and giving away their position.

Strangest thing, Theo thought.

"Pumpkins?"

He'd asked a little too slowly for Alice's liking. "Yes," she said quickly, hoping Theo would catch onto the game.

"Yes."

Good boy.

"Would you like to pick pumpkins with me tomorrow night?" Alice rushed as she crawled back to Theo, staring at him on all-fours.

"Yeah, sure." Theo actually felt a hint of excitement through the anxiousness. Maybe one day he'd be completely cured of his Alice anxiety. And it sounded like pumpkin picking was the next step in that direction.

Unless he had just agreed to pick pumpkins with a crazy person.

Theo blinked as he watched Alice crawl away from him, down the long back hall, and disappear through the exit at the back of the store. Then Grumbles, the giant dog, faithfully mimicked Alice's low crawl and barreled through the door with her.

And that's *the woman you're obsessed with?* Theo thought.

"You've lost your mind," Theo muttered to himself, still sitting on the floor.

"Me too." A dreamy drawl came from around the bookcase.

Theo looked up to see a young man by the name of Noah Clemens. He'd met Noah at Franny's diner when Theo had been trying to win Franny's friendship. Noah was a cook that specialized in scrambled eggs and buttermilk biscuits.

Theo's watched Noah's wistful look as he scanned the tops of the bookcases, and by the time he pushed himself up off the floor, Noah's eyes were on him.

"Hey, Noah," Theo said, finding a bit of humor in the love-struck gaze on the young man's face. "How are you this morning?"

"Hey, Deputy."

Theo decided he liked the sound of his new title.

"I'm looking for a woman. She's beautiful, funny, independent..."

"Ha! Aren't we all, buddy." Theo laughed, wondering if this was how Lane felt when he saw Theo go bonkers around Alice. All gooey, forlorn, and utterly hopeless. It was actually pretty funny.

"Maybe you've seen her?" Noah's eager question seemed desperate.

Theo chuckled. "Hey, anything I can do to help. What's her name?"

"I swear I saw her come in here. Alice. Alice Balfour. You know her, right?" The stars in Noah's eyes turned to meteorites as they shifted from funny-loving to frightful.

"Alice?" Theo asked, hoping he'd heard Noah wrong.

"You do know her! Isn't she the most beautiful woman you've ever seen?"

Yes, she is. Theo thought. *But you can't think that, because I do!*

"Ah," Theo stammered, not knowing what to say. He wanted to tell Noah to take a hike, but what right did Theo have to do that? He didn't have a leg to stand on. Here was Noah, seeking out Alice, looking like he was ready to confess his love, and it took everything Theo had just to agree to pick pumpkins with her.

Theo stared at Noah, who hadn't broken eye contact and who looked like the fate of his future depended on Theo's next words.

"Um, yeah," Theo said, finally. Then he reluctantly pointed in the direction of the back door. "I saw her go that way."

Noah's eyes lit up, and he lunged forward. He wrapped his lanky arms around Theo and gave him a shameless hug. "Thank you! Thank you so much."

Theo wondered if Noah was weeping. But the jealous nausea that was creeping up inside of him trumped all feelings of compassion.

For a split second, Theo contemplated sprinting out the door so he could win the hunt to find Alice. Then he could confess his unrealistic feelings to her before Noah.

But that was exactly why he didn't want to get involved with a woman. He didn't want to compete. He didn't want even the slightest chance of a woman he loved to be interested in another man. And by the looks of it, there was *definitely* another man who was interested in Alice Balfour.

Theo watched Noah race down the hallway. His eyebrows furrowed when he heard Noah yell for him to hear, "Isn't love the most wonderful feeling in the world?"

Theo stood alone in the bookstore with his hands on his hips, trying to figure out what had just happened.

One minute he was confident and offering Alice a hand and accepting a pumpkin date – major progress in his acceptance of feelings for Alice, if he did say so himself. Then the next minute, he was showing a love-crazed guy the way to the very same woman.

Theo needed to decide if Alice Balfour was worth his heart. Because apparently, his wasn't the only heart at stake. He shook his head, then turned to walk back out toward the street and the Fall Festival.

CHAPTER 20

Alice crawled into the back room of her coffee shop with Grumbles as Riley and Paige were laughing in mid-conversation. When she made it all the way in, she closed the door, stood, then wiped at the dirt on her jeans.

"What?" she asked when she looked up and saw both of her friends staring at her and biting their tongues.

Paige led off with huge eyes. "I think I just made the entire town fall in love!" She laughed a little, but tried to reign it in, just in case Alice would be upset at her mixup. "I'm so sorry. I just assumed the little vial was like all the others that we put into our drinks. It was sitting out right next to the cider. I figured you just hadn't gotten around to mixing it in yet. I didn't realize it was for this weeks' batch of lattes. I have to say, it isn't anywhere near as diluted as it usually is." Paige chuckled. "You should have seen it. One sip and eyes glazed over. Incredible."

Alice flopped a hand forward to appear unconcerned - though she felt like she was starting to sweat. "No problem at all." Alice laughed nervously. "A little more love around the town could do some people good."

Zip it! Alice shot the thought over to Riley, who was barely holding her lips together to muffle the laughter that was about to burst out.

"Besides, how many people could have had a cup of cider in that short amount of time?" Alice asked casually, but really, begging for the number to be small. "Three? Five?"

Paige looked toward the ceiling and shifted to casually lean her weight to one foot while counting in her head. *One…five…nine…*

As the number in Paige's mind grew, Alice's eyes swelled as they bore into Riley – who seemed far too excited about the success of the apple cider.

Finally, Paige shrugged, and Alice brought her attention back to the young woman while trying to plaster a casual smile on her face like she'd been waiting patiently for a number the whole time. Not a care in the world.

"Probably twenty-five? Maybe thirty?" Paige said, nodding happily. "I have to say, Alice. Your cider is the perfect Fall Festival drink. It's sweet, tart, crisp, and warm all at once. It's so happy. It's the essence of autumn." Then Paige thought about the rest of the festival. "I suppose we should make more. I think people will really miss it today if we don't have it."

Alice's head just moved up and down in a robotic nod. She had heard Paige but kind of stopped listening when the number of townspeople she thought might have consumed her love potion tallied in the upper twenties.

Riley jumped in for Alice. "What a *great* idea, Paige. You're right. The apple cider would be missed. Maybe Alice and I can whip it up back here. Do you mind running the show out at the festival for the rest of the day? We might be busy."

"I'd love nothing more. It's so happy out there! I *love* this time of the year." Paige dragged out the word *love,* then radiated in the satisfaction from her funny little quip. "See what I did there?"

Riley let out an overzealous laugh and slapped her thigh – mostly for Alice's sake – and received a punishing stare.

"Okay, well. I'll see you gals out there." Paige sauntered out and left Alice and Riley in the back room with a snoring Grumbles.

"You're enjoying this far too much." Alice pointed at Riley.

"That's what best friends – and cousins – are for. To thoroughly enjoy the harmless misfortune that happens to one another. The next time I give a love potion to half the town, I fully expect you to do the same."

"It's twenty-five!" Alice corrected.

"Maybe." Riley shrugged. Then she asked the question that she knew was haunting Alice since her soulmate appeared that morning.

"Do you think Theo drank the cider?"

CHAPTER 21

Two more people had asked Theo about Alice that week. And another didn't ask about her specifically, but if the sketch of Alice – that was the size of the local art gallery window – was any indication of the owner Cole Crawford's feelings, it was safe to say he was another interested party.

If Theo's desire to wander through fields of pumpkins with Alice wasn't so strong, he probably would have written her off as just the type of awful idea he'd rolled into town trying to avoid. But, at the repeated reassurance from Lane and Beck that Alice wasn't a person who pursued multiple love interests – as the scene that was now playing out all over town suggested – he committed to the date.

As a result, Theo was experiencing pre-date jitters.

Would he be judged by the type of pumpkin he picked? Did he need to know more about pumpkins than the near-zero amount he currently did? Should he pick up some carving utensils? All of these things that he hadn't spent two seconds thinking about in his former life now suddenly seemed critical to his existence.

This town was getting to him.

Even with the commotion from the Fall Festival going on outside, the Sheriff's office was quiet, warm, and peaceful. Beck always had a candle burning that smelled and sounded like a crackling bonfire and toasted marshmallows. There was constantly a comforting beverage available, whether it was freshly brewed beans in their office kitchenette or some of Alice's seasonal drinks delivered by the woman herself.

He'd even managed another round of civilized conversation with her earlier that morning.

In fact, *she* had seemed more disheveled than he did. She had been sneaking in and out of the back of their office and constantly looking over her shoulder. And, she'd gotten eerily close to him like she was trying to use him as a human shield. If he hadn't liked it so much, and if the scent of cinnamon and sunflowers on her skin hadn't mesmerized him, he would have found it a bit bizarre.

Theo leaned back in his chair that gave a little with the motion, and he looked around.

He liked it. He more than liked it. And after a night of thinking of the pros and cons of staying, he decided he was going to talk to Lane about making it a permanent position – if the offer was still available.

Even with all of the wacky people, Theo felt this was the place for him. A place he could call home.

As Theo went to take another sip of his latte, the Sheriff's radio crackled as it came to life. The fuzzy sound came and went as clicks from the other end were made.

Lane and Theo moved to stand over the speaker.

"Sheriff? Come in, Sheriff?"

Lane lifted the receiver and pressed the Push To Talk button while looking at Theo. "This is Sheriff Paxon. Go for

Sheriff." Lane lifted his finger off of the PTT button and waited.

"Ah, Sheriff, I think you and Deputy Parker might want to get down to the caramel apple stand."

Lane heard the worry in Nate Newmann – the volunteer safety officer's – voice. "What's going on down there, Nate?"

There were ten seconds of radio silence. And Lane spoke again. "Nate, do you copy?"

"Ahh, yeah. I just, hmm. I don't really know how to describe the issue, Lane."

"Give it your best shot." Lane tried to sound lighthearted and judgment-free to encourage Nate to give them an uninhibited description.

"Well." The radio crackled again. "Um, it seems to be a lovers quarrel. But with three people – I think."

Lane and Theo couldn't help the amused grins they exchanged. "You think?" Lane asked.

"Ah, yeah. It started when Noah Clemens wrote *I LOVE ALICE* in whipped cream on Franny's diner window."

Suddenly the grins fell away.

"That wouldn't have been too big of a deal. But his girlfriend, Stephanie Marsh? Well, she saw it and wasn't too happy. So she started throwing Franny's pumpkin pies from their stand at the window *and* Noah."

"Nate, who's the third person?" Lane asked, wondering if he might need an extra set of 'cuff's should it escalate.

"That's the strange part. I think you might want to talk to Alice."

"Why's that?"

"Well, because Stephanie isn't throwing the pies because Noah is confessing his love for Alice. She's throwin' them because she says she loves Alice more."

"We're on our way." Lane and Theo exchanged one last confused look before quickly getting their gear from their desks and rushing out the front door.

They went on foot because all of Main Street was blocked off for the week-long festival. And because it would have taken longer to run to the cruiser, start it, drive over, and get out than it would have to run across the street and one block over.

Lane and Theo slowed to a jog as they approached.

By the time they got to the scene, a small crowd had started to gather. A three-person lovers quarrel was big news in a small town.

Stephanie shouted that she deserved Alice more than Noah because *she* was the better partner. *She* was the one who made dinners, did the laundry, and cleaned the bathrooms. Noah responded, touting that *he* was the one who painted their rooms the ugly shade of blue and did all the maintenance on their tiny, cottage-style apartment that kept breaking down. *And* apparently, cleaning the bathroom didn't count because it was *the size of a cardboard cereal box.*

The last comment earned Noah a furious look, and another pie hurled in his direction.

"Whoa, whoa, whoa!" Lane and Theo threw themselves into the line of fire. Pies were down like helpless victims all around them, and Franny's window looked like a scene from a horror movie as the whipped cream started to smear, and the words dripped into an illegible creepy jumble of letters.

Both perpetrators were standing with their hands up – which Theo thought was kind of funny. All he and Lane had done was run in between them.

Even the takedowns were cute here, Theo thought with a quick shake of his head.

Just as the thought crossed his mind, Stephanie tried to inch toward another pie at the stand behind her. Lane caught the movement and pointed a decorative cornstalk at her, and said, "Don't even think about it."

Theo tried not to grin or let out the grunt of laughter at the choice of weapon. "Really?" Theo whispered so only Lane, who stood behind him, could hear.

Out of the side of his mouth, Lane responded, "What? It's all that I could reach."

"You're a Sheriff," Theo mumbled back. "You literally have pepper spray, a wand, and a taser."

"A taser? *Really?* Who brings a taser to a…pie fight?" Lane's whisper was a mixture of harsh and *come on, man!*

Theo bobbed his head back and forth, accepting the response. Then Theo made the first move. "Okay. Noah, Stephanie? Why don't you put down the whipped cream can? And no more pies. Let's take this down to the office, and we can talk this through. We'll get Franny and talk about all of…this." Theo circled his finger around the most festive crime scene he'd ever seen.

"And Alice? You'll bring Alice, right?" Noah asked, hopefully.

"But can I talk to her first?" Stephanie then asked, trying to get a leg up on her boyfriend.

Lane shook his head at the bizarre situation. "We need to talk to you two first. Then we'll see who else needs to be involved. Alright," Lane said, motioning for Stephanie to join him in stride. "Let's go."

Theo used his head to motion for Noah to walk with him.

It took ten minutes to get everybody settled. Stephanie was on one end of the conference table, and Noah sat on the other. Both of them had their arms crossed, irritated with one another. It didn't seem worth it to bring them to their own interrogation rooms. Mainly because they only had one, but really…pie-throwing and whipped cream?

"Okay," Lane began. "I need you both – starting with Stephanie – to tell me exactly what's going on."

Stephanie sat straight and proud, then declared, "I'm in love with Alice Balfour."

"That's *not* true!" Noah argued.

Theo looked to Noah for the second time that week and thought he seemed like he was walking around in a haze. "Why is that, Noah?"

"Isn't it obvious?" he asked.

"If you could help explain it to me, it would be very helpful."

"Stephanie can't be in love with Alice." The passion in Noah's voice was adamant.

"Why's that?" Theo needed to hear Noah say it out loud – with other people around, so he didn't feel like he was imagining everything he'd seen this week.

"Because *I'm* in love with Alice Balfour."

Stephanie scoffed and narrowed her eyes at the young man who, just a couple days earlier, was the object of her affection. They had been laughing and swinging hands as they walked into Franny's before Noah started his shift. It didn't make sense. Any of it.

Curious, Theo wondered aloud, "Can you walk me through your days, starting with Monday morning?"

Noah took Lane and Theo through every detail. Starting with waking up next to Stephanie on Monday morning to a perfect fall day straight through until the whipped cream proclamation of love.

Stephanie did the same. Aside from waking up next to each other, going to the first day of the Fall Festival hand-in-hand, and sharing a cup of their favorite – Alice's hot apple cider – they pretty much went their separate ways. And it was apparent, in both of their series of events, the more time they spent apart, the stronger their love for Alice grew. Stephanie had even slept at her mother's house the last two nights.

"Can we trust you two to stay there and not start throwing things at each other?" Lane asked.

When both of the offenders reluctantly nodded, he turned to Beck, who had been pretending not to listen. "You okay out here with these two?"

"You know it," Beck said.

In Lane's office, the men looked at each other, baffled.

"It doesn't make sense," Theo started.

"There was only one thing they did that day that they wouldn't normally have done." Lane made a gesture with his hand that helped support the only possible link.

Both men shrugged and simultaneously said, "The apple cider."

CHAPTER 22

It was *really* hard to avoid people in a small town. Everybody knew where you lived, worked, slept, and everywhere you typically frequented on any given day.

What was worse was Alice had to work, and she had to eat, and she had to sleep. So it's not like she could just stop living.

She'd tried to use magic to help keep the love-struck townspeople at bay, but all it did was reinforce how bad some of her magic was. When she tried to conjure up some fog to make herself hard to see, it started raining on her. And when she tried to make herself blend in with the red brick as camouflage, she accidentally created an image of her face on the brick instead. Things were just not going her way.

And just to be safe, Alice and Grumbles bunked at Riley's house. It wasn't ideal, but it was better than trying to get past the line of people who were waiting for her to come home.

If there was a silver lining to the chaos she'd caused with her misdirected love potion, it was that business was booming. As Alice tiptoed through the shadows of the town just before five in the morning, she peeked around the corner of her building and saw there was already a line forming at the locked door of Witches' Brew. There were also people sitting on the sidewalk, posted up by their festival stand.

Alice pursed her lips as she eyed the crowds. Her coffee was good. But it wasn't *that* good.

"We've got to go through the back, Grumbles," Alice whispered to her loyal companion.

Grumbles gave a low woof – his version of a whisper.

They made it to the back door without being spotted. All seemed safe and quiet until Alice put her key into the lock.

"You've got quite a line out there."

Alice jumped, but she knew the voice. When she looked to the bottom of the stairs that led up the back of the building to her apartment, she saw Theo sitting on the second step.

"Must be something in the cider." Alice shrugged but immediately regretted her choice of words.

Something in the cider! What are you thinking? Alice wanted to slap a hand over her mouth. Could she not lie to him?

The horrible thought sunk in.

Holy. Broomsticks.

It had to be a part of the curse. Or maybe a soul mate thing? Either way, it wasn't good.

"Interesting that you say that." Theo stood and walked over to Alice, who was frozen by the door.

"Want to come in?" Alice ignored the comment and tried to change the subject.

As Theo moved closer, Alice could smell his magnetic spicy scent. It was the encouragement she needed. "Can I make you a latte? We could decide where to meet for pumpkin picking tonight?"

"Sure." Theo nodded as he stared into Alice's blue eyes.

Stay on track. Theo reminded himself. *This* was business. *Tonight* was pleasure.

When Alice turned the key, he reached forward to open the door for her and Grumbles, who paused for a small scratch on his head.

Theo held in the snicker as he watched Alice move slowly along the side of the dark wall, not bothering to turn on a light until they were inside the safety of her back room.

He didn't know what was going on, but he had to admit, as jealous as it made him feel, it was all pretty entertaining, too. And, he also wasn't ashamed to feel a small sense of satisfaction that Alice didn't seem to enjoy the extra attention. In fact, she was doing a good job of avoiding it altogether.

But something *was* going on – and it was his job to find out.

"Do you usually have a line like that? Waiting for you to open?" Theo started to poke his head around the corner to get another look.

The urgency in Alice's voice stopped him. "No! Ah, sorry, no," she said, trying to force a casual tone. "Maybe it's the festival?"

Alice tried to keep her hands busy prepping her work area and for more small talk.

"They *love* the cider. They just keep coming back for more." *Also, not a lie.* "What can I get you to drink? Cider, latte?"

Theo leaned against a small space of an empty wall. It wasn't a big area, but it was cozy and roomy enough. "I think I'll take the one with the maple."

Alice smiled. It was her favorite, too. "That's a very nice choice." She started the easy movements of preparing the espresso and milk for the drink by pulling down the homemade jars of syrups and spices.

"Do you make all of your flavors by hand?" Theo asked, more intrigued with her process than with the case – if it even was a case.

"I do. Of course, not everything can be made by hand. It's easier to buy good Pumpkin Spice than it is to ground all of the spices and mix them together for the amount we need to have on hand this time of the year. But most things, yeah, they're homemade. I think it's a nice, special touch. And of course, it tastes better."

Alice handed Theo the steaming maple latte.

"That, I can't argue with. Thank you." Theo took a hot sip, unable to wait for it to cool. *Delicious.*

Alice wished more than anything she could read Theo's mind. How much simpler it would make the whole situation.

How did people without magical powers survive? It was so hard. Alice was constantly wondering what Theo was thinking and what he was doing. Wanting to know if he was thinking about her. The not knowing was excruciating. Poor humans who had to experience that regularly. Dating would be a nightmare.

Well, she was getting to experience just that because it didn't seem like things were going to change any time soon. She'd have to get to know Theo the good old-fashioned way.

"I shouldn't have assumed you were still interested in picking pumpkins with me. Would you still like to go?" Alice asked, sounding desperately hopeful. "Willa's farm is magical this time of the year."

Magical. Interesting choice of words. Theo was intrigued by all of the mystical qualities of the town – right down to their choice of words. For some odd, utterly irrational reason, he liked it. In any other town, he would have found some of the words they used absolutely ridiculous. But, not here. Because it was magical.

"Yeah, I'd like to see that. Or, to do that with you." And he did. Badly. Almost too badly.

Alice beamed, then watched as Theo mirrored her actions.

That was good, right? A normal person who can't read minds would take his smile as a good sign.

"Great!" Alice tried to bring her voice down an octave. Nobody liked the screechy girl. "Um, great," she tried again, sounding overly casual. "If you want to go together, we could leave from my place – upstairs – around six?"

"I'll drive?" Theo nodded with his suggestion.

"Even better!" Alice couldn't remember being so excited for anything. And she liked that Theo had offered to drive. He was a gentleman. She didn't have to read his mind to see that. But she did wonder, "So, what has you stopping by so early this morning?"

Theo shifted, not knowing how to broach the subject. It was a heck of a lot easier saying ridiculous things to people you weren't actively falling for, dreaming about, etcetera-etcetera.

"Ah, yeah. There was an incident yesterday at the festival in town."

She knew. Alice had heard about it through the small-town rumor mill. But she also knew because Alice could hear the thoughts about her radiating from Noah and Stephanie during their very public lover's quarrel.

Normally, Alice liked to hear people's thoughts. She enjoyed learning about their secret crushes, sassy opinions about who's seeing who, or just random musings about everyday life.

It was entertaining.

Some days she even found it comforting to hear the earnestness of their innermost feelings of love, yearning, and happiness. It helped Alice feel less alone with her own thoughts.

Usually, the passing thoughts came and went, but when the thought was about *yourself,* they flocked to you. Making them not only loud and clear but almost impossible to avoid. There was no amount of covering your ears that would help. You just had to ride out the storm.

"Oh." Alice didn't dare say more. She hoped it sounded like she was curious enough for Theo to explain it himself.

Theo leaned against the wall again. "A couple of people in town got into a bit of an argument. Some property was damaged." Theo couldn't believe he was referring to pumpkin pie as *property*. Only in the town of Lantern Lane…

Theo cleared his throat and said, "Some pies were harmed during the event." He wasn't able to help himself. And he was glad he did. When Alice grinned at his joke, his whole world seemed to make sense. In the scariest, new-relationship way possible.

"Anyway, it was interesting. The two involved seemed to be fighting over a person – not each other."

Was he trying to get her to admit to knowing something about it? Alice tried to move her head side to side, but she was pretty sure she looked like a bobblehead. "Huh. Very peculiar."

"You don't know anything about it, do you?" Theo asked

Alice noticed he seemed more intrigued than interested in accusing her of anything. But she also noticed he hadn't said Stephanie and Noah's names. Was he trying to trick her?

Crap, crap, crap.

Stall. I'm coming. Franny's voice popped into her mind.

Alice's eyebrows raised, knowing Franny was on her way.

Thank all the witches and warlocks for early risers!

"You said pumpkin pies were harmed? How dreadful." Alice choked out the terrible excuse for a hedge, then had to pinch her lips together at how comical it sounded.

"There were."

Thankfully, Theo was playing along.

"It was a terrible waste."

"Alice?" Franny's voice called from the back door. "Are you in here?" Franny asked, knowing with absolute certainty that she was.

Theo and Alice looked toward the sound, then each other.

"Yeah, in here," Alice yelled as if she had no clue Franny was stopping by.

When Franny rushed in, she let the gossip spill, saving Alice. "Alice! Did you hear what happened?"

Alice blinked, *still* unable to respond. Not being able to lie was proving more difficult than she thought. When Franny realized it, she bulldozed on.

"Noah and Stephanie, the *adorable* young couple?" Franny asked, making the point to say Noah and Stephanie's names.

"Of course, I know them."

"Well, they got into it at the festival yesterday. Throwing pies, writing on the diner window. Craziest thing."

Alice felt Theo studying her as she ingested the news. She tried to force her eyes to widen in shock at what she was hearing. She turned her head once or twice to try and show that she was putting the mysterious pieces together. That she realized Franny was talking about the same incident that Theo was. Though Alice was pretty sure she just looked like a big-eyed bug and that her head had a screw loose.

"Anyway," Franny continued. "They were saying they were in love with *you!*"

"With me?" Alice faked the question, and the absurdity of the accusation as her jaw dropped in disbelief. "That's insane." *And it was insane.*

Theo just folded his arms and let the scene play out.

"Are they okay? Are your pies okay?" Alice tried so hard to keep up the show.

Franny almost cracked at the laughable questions. "Yes," she said, barely able to maintain her straight face. "Stephanie and Noah are okay. And the pies, though they'll be missed, can be replaced."

"Okay, you two." Theo pushed away from the wall, shaking his head as both women tried to lay their surprise on as thick as the caramel on Franny's sticky buns. "Let me know if you hear anything that could be of some help to the investigation."

Theo started for the door, nodded at Alice and then at Franny, and said, "Alice. Franny. See you around."

Both women peeked their heads around the corner and watched Theo grin and shake his head on the way out of the back door.

When they pulled themselves back in, Alice wrapped Franny in a hug. "Thank you!"

"Of course. I felt your nerves from all the way across the street." Franny squeezed hard once, then loosened their hug so she could look Alice in the eyes.

"I can't lie to him. And I can't read him. And I can't see where he is when he's not around."

Franny gasped, not realizing the extent of Alice's suffering. Then it hit her. "It must be like being a normal person!"

"It is!" Alice felt relieved that somebody else understood what she was going through.

"Is it awful?" Franny asked, wanting to know more.

"The worst. I don't know how non-magical people do it. Dating must be a terrible experience."

"I don't even want to imagine. Well," Franny said, after a moment, "are you making any progress?" Of course, she was asking about Theo.

Alice blushed and smiled like a schoolgirl with a crush. "We're going to Willa's pumpkin patch tonight to pick pumpkins."

"Fantastic. Can I help?"

Alice thought about it, then the idea came. "Can I order a picnic dinner from the diner?"

Franny grinned. "I have just the meal for you."

CHAPTER 23

Theo hadn't gotten much further with the lover's quarrel case, aside from the fact that three more people had come forward stating they were witnesses to the argument. *And* that the argument had no merit.

When Theo had asked each of them why he distinctly remembered wanting to bang his head against the red brick of the wall when they said it was because *they* were the ones who were *actually* in love with Alice.

Three men, two women– all claiming unending love for Alice – and the only thing they all had in common was they lived in Lantern Lane, and all of them had indulged in the apple cider the first morning of the Fall Festival.

Unless there was something in the water. And there wasn't a report in the world Theo was going to write that on. The people of Lantern Lane were simply losing their minds. All of them. At the same time.

But, even crazier than all of the people confessing their love was that, on some, deranged, not at all logical level, he *understood* how they felt. Because at any given time of the day, *he* thought of Alice – awake or dreaming. And what was worse, as each of his witnesses came forward, professing love, *he* wanted to tell them that *he* was the one who was in love with Alice.

"Just not even rational, man," Theo whispered the words to himself at his desk as he stared at the statements he'd taken earlier in the day.

Without thinking about his actions, Theo lifted up the latte he'd splurged on that afternoon and inhaled the scent of cinnamon before taking a sip. It smelled of Alice, of her coffee shop, of the town.

He had arrived expecting to get time alone, some quiet. Time to be a single man. To regroup and settle into a nice, quiet period of bachelorhood while hanging out with his old buddy on a new job.

Instead, the instant he pulled into town, he was drawn to a woman he'd never met. He started experiencing feelings he swore to himself he'd never feel again.

"Hey Theo, are you heading home soon?"

"Ah, no. I'm heading to a pumpkin patch."

"That sounds like fun. What brings you there?"

Theo looked up. "If you can't beat 'em, join 'em. Or something like that."

Beck rested a hip on Theo's desk and gave him a satisfied grin. "Mind if I ask what exactly you're joining in on?"

Theo dropped his head. "I can't believe I'm even saying this. I–" Theo swallowed, then lifted his eyes to Beck. "I'm going to try and get Alice Balfour to fall in love with me."

"Ah," Beck said, giving a knowing nod. "Decided to drink the Kool-Aid?"

"I think in this case, it's more like apple cider."

"If the pointy shoe fits." Beck lifted herself up and crossed the room. She yelled goodbye to Lane, then grabbed her fall jacket and bag, and walked into an evening that – to nobody's surprise – seemed like the perfect autumn night.

After a bit of rustling around, Theo saw Lane walk out of his office and toss on his own jacket. Lane paused for a second in the middle of the room and looked at Theo.

Their staring contest only lasted as long as Theo allowed it to. "Spit it out," he said, finally.

"It's about time." Lane's satisfied grin stretched across one side of his face.

"It's literally been a little over a week." Theo reminded Lane.

"Well, when you know, you know. You know?" Lane shrugged.

Theo pointed to the door. "You should…you know…go."

Lane laughed and left Theo alone.

Theo liked to think he was an uncomplicated, confident man. That he didn't care what people thought of his looks or his clothes. Heck, for more than half his life, he'd been sporting a blue or brown uniform. It didn't necessarily require him to put much thought into impressing anybody.

Theo drummed his fingers the top of his desk, and his foot popped up and down like he had a nervous tick. After a minute of contemplation, Theo looked down at his uniform and assessed.

"For the record, you *are* uncomplicated and confident," Theo reassured himself in the emptiness of the office. "But, nobody goes pumpkin picking in a uniform, right?"

The clock on the wall told him he had thirty minutes until he was due at Alice's apartment above the coffee shop.

At the thought, Theo pushed away from his desk and rushed out the door. It's not like he was trying to upstage everybody else who was pursuing Alice…*oh, heck.* Why try and deny it?

He wanted to look good, and he wanted Alice to notice.

The problem with being a man who'd sworn off women was that when you made a move to another location – in this particular case, to a smaller town where you thought you'd only see a buddy and the occasional old woman to help across the road – you packed one shirt that kind of passed as a *dating shirt,* and your jeans looked like they've been through every form of car maintenance, house repair, and lawn care service imaginable.

Theo stared at his reflection in the bathroom mirror and blinked.

Not good. Very not good.

After one more look at himself, Theo decided he needed help. His phone was under the pile of clothes – all two shirts and one additional pair of jeans. When he found it, he scrolled through his contacts and clicked Lane's name.

"Hey, shouldn't you be picking up Alice right about now?" Lane didn't bother with formalities, just jumped right into a conversation.

"I…need help?" It was all Theo could manage.

"Flowers." Lane's response was simple.

"Sorry…what?"

"The answer is always *flowers.*"

"But I'm talking about–" Theo was cut off.

"Flowers."

"You're killing me." Theo rubbed a hand down his face. This was a waste of time.

"Listen. It's simple," Lane began. "You're meeting the family: flowers. You're sorry for something: flowers. You don't want her to notice the huge volcano-sized zit on your forehead: flowers."

Theo heard the satisfaction of an explanation well-presented on Lane's end. Lane was feeling proud. Theo just rolled his eyes.

"So, it looks like I stole my outfit off of a scarecrow."

"One word, my friend," Lane said.

Irritated, Theo said the word at the same time as Lane.

"Flowers."

"Yeah, yeah. Got it." Theo paused, thinking about what he had to do. Then he nodded. "Right. Uh, gotta go, then."

"Make me proud!"

Theo heard the shout through the phone as he lowered it, then clicked out of the call. He looked around for his wallet, swooped it up, then ran out of his apartment. He had ten minutes.

Thank goodness for small towns. Theo was at the florist in under two minutes. He made good time, considering he had to dodge people loitering about at the Fall Festival and saying *hi* to each one of them. Because Theo learned, you had to acknowledge every living being you walked by - including the animals.

Thankfully, upon entering the flower shop, he was the only one in line. Apparently, everybody in town was in good standing with their significant others.

"Be right there!"

Theo grinned while he quickly gauged how he was doing on time.

So far, so good, He thought. *And, the flowers will be worth it.*

When Joshua Stems – Theo still had to try and hold himself together at the unfortunate, or, maybe fortunate, name – walked into the front of the store with a monstrosity of a vase filled with flowers, he felt there was no way he could leave disappointed.

"Hey, Theo," Josh said as he set the vase down with a thud. "What can I do for you?"

"I'm hoping to pick up some flowers. Uh, for a woman." Theo tried again, "Actually, for a date."

Josh smiled, looking like he'd seen the nervous stance and the unsure request before. "We've got what you need. Do you have something in mind, or would you like me to throw something together?"

"Ahh." Theo knew as much about flowers as he did about the woman he was trying to impress with them. He knew she was beautiful and that she seemed nice, but aside from that, nada.

"How about I throw something together, and you can guide me along by answering a couple of questions."

Theo breathed a sigh of relief. "That sounds like you're saving my life."

The laugh from Josh was easy as he rounded the corner and moved toward the wall of refrigerators that held so many flowers Theo wouldn't even have known where to start.

"Okay, let's start with: seasonal or occasional?"

"First date, but she loves the season." So far, he was killing it.

Josh nodded and moved in front of the door that had reds, oranges, pinks, purples, and peach-colored flowers.

"First date." Josh thought about it for a minute. "How does she make you feel?"

Oh boy, maybe this was going to be more challenging than he thought.

"Um, she's perfect. She's beautiful and bright. She's fun, and I think she's funny. A little quirky – but in a good way."

"You seem pretty smitten for a first date." Josh spoke as he pulled different flowers out of different buckets."

Theo's head fell as he chuckled, becoming a bit more comfortable with his discomfort about his love situation. "I am not ashamed to admit that I would do just about anything to make this woman fall in love with me." Then Theo looked up, "But, if you ask me to explain *that*, I'm going to have to leave you empty-handed."

Josh laughed again. "I know how you feel. You know? Chances are, I know who she is. Maybe I can toss in her favorite flower."

"That'd be great!"

Flowers. Who knew? Theo mused, mentally taking note to congratulate Lane on his great idea.

"Alice. Alice Balfour. In fact, I'm sure you know her." Because everybody knew everybody.

Josh's smile faded instantly. He walked to the trash and dropped all of the stems he'd just picked in to meet their doom at the bottom of the large gray basket.

Without another word, Josh moved to the fridge at the front of the store, pulled open the door, and picked a worthless, too many days old, dying bouquet out of a bin that had a sign touting *70 Percent Off!*

The large whites of Theo's eyes followed a different version of Josh as his actions were choppy and deliberate. Finally, when Josh stopped in front of the door, holding the pathetic-looking flowers, Theo took a tentative step toward them.

"Take them, and go," Josh said, trying to keep whatever was left of his professionalism intact.

Theo inched forward. "Josh? Is everything okay?" Slowly, Theo reached his hand forward to take the bouquet and snatched them away before the *new* Josh changed his mind.

Josh opened the door to his shop and pointed a finger so close to Theo's nose his eyes crossed as they focused on the tip.

"You might be the lucky guy that gets to date Alice tonight. But I'll have you know, I don't intend to go down without a fight."

Theo side-stepped through the door opening and stood on the sidewalk as Josh let the door slam closed between them. He watched as Josh pointed two fingers from his eyes to Theo's. The good old *I'm watching you* gesture. Then Josh did an about-face and marched away from him.

"What the heck?!" Theo said while sneaking a glance at his watch.

He made a mental note to send Lane back to the shop to interview Josh - obviously, he wouldn't get too far with the florist at this point. But there had to be something he was missing.

But right now, he had somewhere to be.

KATIE BACHAND

CHAPTER 24

The drive to the pumpkin patch was enchanting. The seasonal shift in the sun had dusk settling in at an early hour and a rustic brown tone filtering the golden fields, with orange and green pumpkins scattered across it. Glowing amber lights were strung down the length of a dirt path that led from a small barn to the entrance of the field. They weren't needed, as the purple and orange colors of the sunset were still holding on, but they offered a magical, romantic glow.

Alice felt the burn of Theo's glances while they walked. The vulnerability she felt, and the new and exotic way it made her feel, was fascinating. And when their eyes caught once or twice, she couldn't help the blushing smile as the innocence of the moment consumed her.

Everything about Theo was unexpected and spectacular. The way he'd insisted on carrying the basket of food Franny had packed for their date. And how he tried to get her to leave the poor, wilted excuse of a bouquet behind in his truck. But, even then, he gave in when she touched his hand and reassured him they were beautiful, and she said she had just the place for them.

He was entirely new. From the way he rolled into town unexpectedly to the way she had been drawn to him.

In a way, she was grateful her magic was useless. The complicated way it forced her to navigate their feelings for one another was agonizingly wonderful.

As the dirt path curved around one end of the pumpkin patch, a picnic table came into view. Both Alice and Theo felt the excitement of the exquisite scene.

The surprise lit up Alice's eyes, and Theo looked at her and asked, "Did you do all of this?"

Alice laughed and shook her head, then ran the last few feet and stood in front of the table.

"Willa," Alice said lovingly. She looked at Theo, who had joined her. "Willa must have done this."

And Alice knew she had. She felt the essence of the magic Willa had left behind. It was like smelling the smoke from a candle that had just been blown out. It lingered.

Alice closed her eyes and felt the actions Willa had taken to light the candles that were clustered in the middle of the table. She felt the magic Willa had used to spiral the leaves that had fallen from the trees around the farm. The push and pull to have them scatter the ground beneath the table. And, the fresh scent of sweet and spice told Alice that Willa had used her breath to blow the essence of apples and cinnamon across the table so it would linger in the air.

Then there was everything that didn't require magic but required time and attention. Willa had draped maroon and gold plaid blankets on the dining benches for warmth when the sun finally fell out of the sky. She'd lit a fire for heat and for the romantic sound it made as the wood snapped and embers sparked into the evening sky.

It was perfect.

Alice giggled a bit. She was giddy! How glorious.

When Theo playfully bumped her with his elbow and held up the basket, she laughed.

"Should we dive in?" His brown eyebrows rose with the question.

Alice could have sworn he was just as excited as she was. She nodded and said, "Absolutely."

The basket was filled with the fragrant scent of fall. Roasted butternut squash soup topped with salty pumpkin seeds, cheesy grilled sandwiches wrapped in parchment and tied with string, and slices of apple and pumpkin pie for dessert were all expertly fitted into the basket. A bottle of wine was rolled into a towel and tucked into the side. And an empty mason jar with a little note inside sat on the top. Alice pulled out the paper and read it aloud.

"Enjoy!" She tilted the paper and leaned into Theo so he could read it for himself.

She set the jar in the middle of the old wooden table, filled it with the water that had been set out for them, and put the flowers Theo had given her in the center. She couldn't use magic on Theo, but the curse didn't mention anything about flowers.

While Theo was setting the empty basket on the ground next to their table, Alice quickly folded her hands around the petals and lifted them, causing fresh blooms to sprout with the movement.

They settled in, each taking a seat on one side of the table so they could face the open field and the barns in the distance.

Theo grinned as they took their first sips of soup.

"What?" Alice asked, feeling self-conscious.

"Nothing." Theo shrugged. "Just wishing this night would have been my idea."

Alice laughed and thought it was sweet that he'd even take the time to think about something like that.

"I needed pumpkins," she said. "And I'll need more. How about you plan the next one?" She knew the question sounded eager, but she also didn't know how long she had before whatever the curse happened to be took effect.

"Deal." Theo nodded before crunching into the buttery, toasted sandwich. "Are the pumpkins for decorating?" He asked while trying to keep his mouth closed.

"Among other things." Alice grinned. "Are you interested in hearing what for?"

"I have to tell you the truth. I've never been more interested in a pumpkin in my life." He wasn't lying. Theo wanted to know everything that Alice found interesting. If it happened to be a pumpkin, then he wanted to know about pumpkins.

A freaking pumpkin! Theo thought. If that wasn't the onset of love, he didn't know what was.

"Well then, okay." Alice couldn't remember the last time she was able to talk about her business with anybody. Or, maybe, the last time she *wanted* to.

"A pumpkin is so much more than a cute – or scary – decoration. And, though they are perfection in a pumpkin pie, their benefits are plenty." Alice grinned and took a slurp of her squash soup.

"Very intriguing," Theo led her on. "Tell me more."

"I feel like I need to give a prelude to what I'm about to tell you because you might get the wrong idea about me."

Theo's laugh was easy.

"I was *not* a good student. But, I did love science. And it kind of stuck." *It's probably why I'm so good at potions,* Alice thought.

"So, if I use words like Vitamin A, Beta Carotene, folate, and Vitamin C – which are all found in pumpkin – know that the brainpower mostly applies only to science."

Impressed, Theo said, "I'll take your word for it." Then he added, "But I'm still impressed; I wasn't even good at science."

"No?" Alice couldn't help but wonder what Theo was like in school.

"Nope, I was all about physical education." He nodded. "I was the kid whose favorite class was *gym.*"

"That's adorable," Alice admitted.

"Why, thank you. But this isn't about me. Hit me with the pumpkins." Theo leaned in to listen and for another bite of crusty sandwich.

Totally adorable. Alice swooned as she watched, thoroughly entertained at the easy way Theo had settled in with her. Like he'd forgotten that only a few days ago, he was avoiding her. But then again, she supposed it could all be fake. Eventually, the love potion would wear off.

Alice looked at Theo. *Really* looked.

She couldn't see inside of him, but she could memorize his face. The way his jaw clenched with every bite. The way his ears lifted slightly when he smiled. The stubble that found its way to his face by the end of every day. If this time with him had to come to an end, she wanted to remember every detail.

"Everything okay?" Theo asked, giving her a funny look.

Alice gave a small smile. She couldn't nod – she tried – but apparently, the higher witch powers thought that would have been a lie. So instead, she lifted a small, decorative pumpkin from the table and held it up. "At this little pumpkin's core, it is a germ-fighting, immune-system-boosting champion."

That's when it clicked for Theo. "Ahh," he said. "Your drinks. That's how you provide all of those extra benefits in your drinks."

Alice nodded, knowing it was a bit more than that, but it was true enough.

They ate in comfortable silence for a little bit. But the sun was starting to fall, and they were losing what was left of daylight.

"Are you ready?" Alice asked.

"For what?" Theo had forgotten that this date wasn't only to sit and stare at the object of his affection.

"We need to pick some pumpkins."

"Let's do it."

Theo lifted his legs over the bench and started to move around the table to help Alice up, but she was too quick. She'd already slid out and grabbed the handle of the rickety wagon that had been left by the table.

Alice led the way into the fields and breathed in the fresh air. Getting to walk through the fields, select the vegetables, pick the fruits, and clip the herbs for her shop's beverages was one of the best parts of her job.

They walked for a bit, enjoying the quiet, stopping every once in a while for Alice to pick up a pumpkin then set it down; or to lift it, show it off to Theo, then plop it in the wagon when they both agreed it was perfect.

Alice stole a sideways glance in Theo's direction as they made their way down another row.

"What?" Theo asked, feeling her stare.

"Am I allowed to ask about your bad relationship on a first date?"

Theo lifted a single brow and looked intrigued. "Is this a date?"

Alice couldn't stop the blush. "I suppose it is if you want it to be one."

"Yeah." Theo nodded. "I want it to be one."

Inside, Alice felt fireworks bursting all around. Her heart danced in a circle and had to have doubled in size. But she managed – barely – to nod coyly. "Then it's a date."

"Then sure, you can ask." Theo took the time to reach over and grab the handle of the wagon, so he could begin pulling it for Alice since she'd successfully stacked it into an impressive mound.

Alice bumped him with her shoulder to encourage him to talk.

Theo shrugged. "There's not much to tell, really. She found interests outside of our relationship – two of them were other men. Like I said before, I'm old-fashioned. I like to think when two people commit to each other, they're in it for the long haul."

"It hurt." Alice said the words for Theo.

He nodded again, then agreed, "It hurt."

Theo pulled the wagon the rest of the way back to their picnic table and pulled the blankets off the benches. He motioned to the chairs sitting around the fire, and Alice agreed.

When she sat, he draped the blanket over her; then, he took a seat in the chair next to hers and did the same to himself.

"I moved here to get away from women."

Alice let Theo's admission sink in. Then the hysterics got the best of her. She started laughing so hard, she had to hold her stomach. Her head fell back, and her eyes closed.

Theo accepted the laughter. He nodded and even joined her for a bit.

"I'm sorry," Alice gasped through the tears. "It's just…there are *so many* women here."

Theo hunched over and laughed again. It was funny because it was true. He couldn't have picked a worse town to try to avoid women in.

Alice pressed her sore cheeks as she tried to regain her composure. "I really am sorry. But it explains *a lot.*" She couldn't tell him about the curse, but wouldn't it be just her luck.

"Oh, does it?" Theo looked at the most beautiful woman in the world, squeezing her face and looking absolutely ridiculous. She was perfect.

Alice nodded. "Oh, yeah. Leave it to me to not care about a single man my whole life, then find myself attracted to the one man who's written off women."

Bridget, her great, great, great, great – whatever she was – sure had a sick sense of humor.

Theo forgot all about his embarrassment. "So, what you're saying is, you like me?"

Alice wasn't ready for the second round of sore cheeks. *"That's* what you're taking away from all of this?"

"It's the only thing I want to." Theo was serious then.

And, for that moment, both of them started to think there was more than a little bit of hope.

CHAPTER 25

Two blissful days of sneaking away for back-alley coffee breaks, quick chats on the phone, and one *so sweet* surprise bouquet of dying flowers left on her doorstep, had Alice feeling like the curse couldn't be real. Things were going too wonderfully to think otherwise.

"You call this *wonderful?*" Riley asked as they squatted behind a mailbox, then slid behind a slow-moving van as it backed into a delivery zone in front of Riley's book store. "You're sneaking around town like a deranged spy."

Alice and Riley hit their knees when they saw Mrs. Hendricks loitering around the coffee shop window. Her face and hand were pressed against the glass as she tried to peer into the dark, empty space.

Riley rolled onto her butt to rub her sore knees. "For goodness sakes, at least use your magic to help with some of this stuff."

Alice reached into her bag and held out a lotion potion.

"What's this?" Riley asked.

Alice motioned in the direction of Riley's knees. "Use it on your old-lady knees."

"This is the best you've got?" Riley asked accusingly.

Alice rolled her eyes, then sat next to Riley. "Yes. Because yesterday when I tried to make it foggy to hide from Noah, I made it rain again. My hair gets frizzy in the rain."

"Your hair gets frizzy in the rain." Riley stared at Alice. *"That's* what you're going with?"

Alice shrugged. "And, Grumbles smells when he gets wet."

"You're hopeless. You *know* what you need?"

"Don't go there."

"You know what you need," Riley said flatly.

"I don't want to talk about it." Alice tried to brush off the suggestion.

"They'd help."

"They drive me crazy."

The loud *woof* that came from inside of the bookstore brought the two witches back to reality. They realized they were both sitting on the brick sidewalk, out in the open. The van had moved, and with Grumbles barking, the commotion would draw attention.

"Alice?" Mrs. Hendricks turned at the scuffle and squinted her eyes the length of the block between them. "Alice!"

"Go, go, go!" Alice said, pushing Riley toward the door.

"Alice, wait!" Mrs. Hendricks was doing her best to move quickly, but years of too many slices of pie and sweet potato stew weren't helping the sweet round woman. She waved her hand as she waddled down the sidewalk.

"Mrs. Hendricks?" Theo asked as he stepped out of the Sheriff's Office just in time to see the old woman droop when Alice had disappeared into the store.

"I love you." Mrs. Hendricks let the wistful whisper slide out. The longing in her voice sounded desperate and hopeless.

"Mrs. Hendricks?" Theo tried again. "Can I help you?"

The old woman, who had been so kind to him when he moved into town, furrowed her brows and pointed a crooked finger at him. "Don't you play coy with me, Mr. Parker. I know you've been trying to steal Alice away from me. I've got my eye on you." Mrs. Hendricks walked away, muttering, "These young wiper-snappers think they can swoop in and charm Alice with their ruggedly handsome good looks."

Theo couldn't believe it. Mrs. Hendricks, too? If it hadn't been ridiculous – or seriously affecting the town – it would have been a lot funnier. But he supposed since everything was going so well for him with Alice, it was easier to see the humor.

He turned and walked right back into the office he'd just left and yelled, "Lane, we've got another one!"

Alice and Riley hid in the bookstore for the next hour, talking and laughing. Alice thought these quiet times, where they were literally forced to hide away, were kind of nice.

They were both sitting behind the checkout counter with their backs on the floor and their feet sticking straight up in the air, resting on the cabinets.

Alice turned her head to the side to look at Riley and said, "He's everything I could have ever wanted in a partner –

in a man. He's sweet, caring, chivalrous. He's funny and honest. He even asked me about pumpkins."

Alice laughed as she thought back to their perfect fall first date – which *was* a date – as they ever so cutely agreed it was.

Riley grinned, but it was timid and reserved.

Alice mirrored the look. "What is it?"

Riley took Alice's hand. "I love seeing you like this. I love that you found your soulmate. But I want you to be careful."

Alice turned her head to stare at the ceiling. She knew what Riley meant. She'd been pushing the feelings of hesitation away, avoiding the inevitable.

"Aren't you just a little bit worried the reason Theo is perfect is because of the love potion he drank? Or," Riley hesitated, not wanting to say the following words out loud, but they couldn't be avoided, "that the curse might end up hurting you and Theo – or worse?"

The quiet was all the answer Alice needed to give and that Riley needed to hear. They both knew the curse couldn't be ignored and that the potion had to be dealt with.

Alice covered her face with her hands as if she was hiding from the truth behind them.

"I can't believe I'm about to say this." Her words sounded low and muffled from the barrier.

"But?" Riley didn't want to snicker, but she was about to hear something that Alice had never said before.

Alice moaned, then grunted. "I need to go see the aunts again."

The words felt like torture. And Grumbles felt her agony. The big dog scooted closer to Alice and rested his gigantic head on her tummy, and whimpered.

"At least Grumbles gets me," Alice said while rubbing the soft fur on Grumbles' head.

Then Riley lifted herself to her elbow, the quick motion screaming that she had an idea.

Alice turned her head again, not ready for the excitement. "What is it?" Alice asked, suddenly feeling exhausted with the idea of going to visit the aunts in seek of help.

"What if you brought him?" Riley moved all the way up and sat cross-legged next to Alice.

"What are you talking about?" Even though Alice *knew* what Riley was talking about.

"What if you *bring* Theo…you know, to the aunts?"

"Are you nuts?" Alice lifted herself to her elbows and eyed Riley. "He doesn't even know I'm a witch. I can't subject him to three of the battiest people I know."

"Come on, they're not *that* bad."

Alice pursed her lips. "They literally wear all black gowns and matching pointy hats. The only reason they don't wear the funny-looking boots is because they are adamant about walking around barefoot like their cherished ancestors would have most likely done."

Riley shrugged, not willing to accept that those qualities made their aunts crazy.

"Riley," Alice sounded serious. "They chant *buck naked* on the winter solstice."

"I mean, sure. That part is a little weird."

"You're a lost cause." Alice laid back down.

"No." Riley took Alice's hand again. "I'm trying to believe in yours."

Alice squeezed Riley's fingers. "I know. I'm just not willing to risk whatever good Theo and I have going – at least not right now."

"Okay." That much, Riley understood. "What's your next move?"

Alice breathed again. "Well, he's coming over for dinner and apple cider making."

Riley was entertained. "Does he know that?"

The sly smile caused Riley to grin. "He knows about dinner."

"You're playing with fire."

"Oh, there'll be fire all right," Alice admitted. "I want Theo to see how it's done so he understands that it couldn't possibly have been my apple cider that caused the town to go wacky."

"Even though it was?"

"Not the point," Alice reiterated. "Technically, it was the potion, not the cider."

"Playing with fire!" Riley sang.

CHAPTER 26

At the knock on her apartment door, Alice held her arms straight out to the side, then slowly lowered them. When she did, the feather-duster settled onto the ground, the vacuum turned off and folded into its upright position, the music softened to gently fill the quiet, and the oven temperature lowered to a nice warm so their dinner wouldn't burn.

Alice quickly picked up the duster and dragged the vacuum to her closet – some things just worked better when you used your hands – then she yelled, "Hello! Coming!"

Before opening the door, she did one final spin, assessing her apartment. The air was fresh, with a fall breeze flowing through the open window. It smelled like the savory beef stew that was warming in the oven, and the crackling fire and the cozy throws draped over her furniture made it look cozy and inviting.

She nodded, then swung open the door.

Alice knew her smile was too big, too excited, and far too attracted to Theo. If she hadn't closed her mouth, she might have salivated.

THE PROBLEM WITH LOVE POTIONS

She would give her first spellbook to know what he was thinking.

Theo Parker stood, framed by her doorway, in what looked to be a brand-new outfit. The navy-blue flannel was crisply ironed but casually left unbuttoned at the top. And, he was adorably holding a beautiful burgundy bottle of wine.

How was it possible she hadn't realized how deep the blue of his eyes were until now? And wasn't it funny – and she suspected the potion had something to do with it – that their outfits kind of matched. She'd chosen a light blue chambray shirt for herself and tucked it into some dark form-fitting jeans.

"You're beautiful," Theo said as a thrilling new spark found its way into them.

I'm melting. As a witch, the humor of the thought wasn't lost on her.

"So are you," Alice said, wondering if he was feeling the same attraction to her as she was to him.

"Come in." Alice stepped to the side and let him walk inside.

The way his shoulders immediately rose and fell, as if his whole body relaxed, had Alice hoping it felt like coming home to him.

Theo looked around the room, taking it in, enjoying the comfort. Then his eyes settled on a small entry table, and his face fell.

Traitor. He thought, remembering the enormous bouquet Josh had been working on days earlier.

On the table was the ridiculous monstrosity of flowers. Theo shouldn't have felt protective, but what guy *really* doesn't care if another man is sending his love interest flowers?

Alice saw the glint of competition in Theo's eyes. She didn't want to…but she did. "Oh, do you like them?" She walked to the table.

Playing with fire. Riley's words slammed into her mind.

Luckily, Theo saved her from herself. "Josh." Theo shook his head and finally smiled. "He sent me away with the flower equivalent of a mushy jack-o-lantern. And he sent you the prize pumpkin."

Alice's heart beat quickly as she gazed adoringly at him. He was perfect. He was her soulmate. There wasn't a doubt in her mind. If only it didn't take a love potion to make him feel it too.

She nudged his shoulder and felt the sparks from the touch. "If it's any consolation prize, the flowers from you are the only ones I care about."

Taking a chance, Theo linked his fingers with hers. She knew it was a risk for him. And when they held, Alice closed her eyes, knowing he was feeling the same burn, the same spark.

But she wondered, did he feel the way it weaved through her body like the feeling of savoring a warm drink? Did it make him want to wrap his arms around his body to hold onto the feeling? Did it make him long for that feeling every day, for the rest of his life?

"You're an amazing woman, Alice Balfour." He squeezed her hand lightly, then was the first to break the connection.

When he let go and moved into her apartment, she did hold herself. It had been six days since Theo had drunk the potion.

Alice wondered how many more moments like this they'd have. How many willing touches, how many pretty words, before the potion would wear off, and Theo would remember that he was trying to avoid her?

Or, worse yet, how long did they have before whatever pain and punishment of the curse would take effect?

At least when the potion wore off, he'd still be here. If she could still see him, there was still hope. But, the curse could do everything from banishing him from her life…or worse.

Alice shivered. She couldn't think of *worse*.

"Hey, are you okay?" Theo asked from across the room. "You look like you just saw a ghost."

"Huh." Alice found the unintentional humor a little untoward. And she couldn't get herself to make a joke about it. Because the reality of it was if the curse was anything like the scary – but true – stories she'd been told as a young witch, the ghost could be Theo's soon enough.

Alice forced a smile. "Yup, all good."

The longer Theo was in the apartment, the more he felt like he belonged there. He could easily imagine waking up there every day, heading in to work with Alice, picking up a coffee from her shop along the way. Then after a day of work, walking around town, keeping whatever peace was left to be kept, then coming home to Alice and sharing a dinner like they had that evening.

The apartment wasn't big. The living area had a fireplace, a single chair, and a couch. The TV was small – something that he might have to bargain with her on – but it was clean and cozy. It was nice, but it felt lived in. Alice had little trinkets and picture frames sitting on shelves and side tables. Books were scattered around the room, some in a small bookcase and others stacked on an ottoman.

Theo could easily imagine sitting next to the fire at night, reading a book, with Alice's feet propped on his lap. Every once in a while, they'd think of something that happened from their day, talk and laugh about it, then settle back into their stories – all with Grumbles sleeping, and probably snoring, at his feet.

"I'd give just about anything to know what's going through your mind right now." Alice looked over the top of her wine at Theo and his wandering eyes as she took a sip. *And she really would give anything.*

Theo shrugged. How did he tell the woman of his dreams he had mentally moved in with her after only two to three solid days of dating? In his defense, a dating article he'd read mentioned that a man knows in the first ten seconds of meeting a woman if he wants to see her again. He wondered if that applied to love, marriage, and the rest of your life with another person?

This probably wasn't the time to discuss the details, but he could share a little.

"I was thinking it would seem pretty nice to kick my feet up over by the fire and settle in for the evening. Do you do it often?"

Very nice, Theo thought, feeling confident in his delivery.

"I do. Every night. Some days I don't even read. I just pop open one of my coffee table books," *or a potions book,* she thought, "and just thumb through, looking at the pictures while enjoying the fire and the not-so-subtle sound of Grumbles' dreams."

"Yup," Theo agreed. "Pretty much exactly like I imagined it."

How cute is that? As if she needed more of a reason to love him. But not tonight.

"But," she lifted her pointer finger off of her wine glass and angled it in Theo's direction, "not tonight. We're going to do an activity together."

"Oh really?" Theo asked, lifting his own wine glass to take a sip.

"Really. You were asking me the other day about my apple cider. So I thought it would be fun if we made it together." Alice lifted her shoulders in a way that asked, *what do you think?*

Theo couldn't deny he was interested in it. And, it would put to rest the apple cider theory. But mostly, it was a heck of a good excuse to stay a bit longer with her.

"I should warn you. It takes a while."

"For you, I've got nothing but time."

Alice thought, *Let's hope so.*

She grinned at Theo – who was now wearing an apron that matched hers – as they sliced a mixture of sweet and tart, red and green apples. They'd already set out all of the spices and made sure to bask in the fragrant wonder of each one: the long cinnamon sticks, the round balls of clove, the magical anise stars, and the earthy look of the nutmeg. Next, they peeled the oranges and zested a lemon.

When their busy bodies warmed from the movement and the fire, rather than put out the blaze that offered the perfect ambiance to the moment, they simply threw the window open and let the wind whip through the small kitchen.

Alice didn't know it at the time, but when Theo slammed his last apple and the peeler on the counter and yelled, "Time!" she picked up on the fact that they'd been racing.

Men. Alice thought as she playfully rolled her eyes and threw her head back, and laughed.

She tossed him a damp towel for his sticky hands when she finished, then Alice put her hands on her hips.

"What's next?" Theo asked, feeling accomplished and more invested in the fall season than he'd ever been.

Alice didn't know if he was ready – or if she was ready – for what she was about to do next.

"We cook. And we wait." Alice nodded, trying to stall. It was moments like these she wished she would have had the foresight to buy a normal pot. Some nice non-stick canning pot or one of those oversized French Dutch ovens that were all the craze. But then again, she'd never needed one. So, here she was, about ready to whip out a cauldron. Which, by the way, she'd never had to move without magic.

Alice was still nodding, half thinking and half trying to convince herself to speak. Finally, she just had to go for it. "I'm going to need your help."

"Name it."

He was so easy.

"Follow me."

Alice tapped her foot and rested her hands on her hips, giving the action one more contemplation, then she looked at Theo, turned toward the closet door, reached for the knob, and pulled.

There it was. A colossal witch's cauldron. Big. Black. And probably weighed a bazillion pounds.

Alice tried to spy on Theo out of the corner of her eye and noticed even Grumbles was interested enough in the show to flop his head backward and watch for himself.

"Is that a–" Theo pointed to the cauldron.

"Yup. Yes, it is. We really get into the season around here."

Theo bobbed his head. They really did go all out for the season. And, surprisingly, it wasn't the strangest thing he'd seen in the last couple of weeks.

Theo clapped his hands, ready to move on. "Okay, how do we get it out?"

"How do we get it out?" Alice repeated, then said it again to herself as she thought about how to maneuver it without magic. "How *do* we get it out?"

Theo examined it. "I can't believe you do this by yourself. Do you roll it?"

"I roll it!" Alice exclaimed, delighted with the idea.

"Great, let's do it. Glad I'm here to help."

"You and me, both." Alice snuck a glance at Grumbles, who rolled his eyes and rested his head on his paws to keep watching.

Because the enormous base was round, they ended up spinning it in circles across the floor until they reached the fireplace. Luckily her cousins had helped her install the hook into her old stone fireplace, so using the crank to latch to the top of the pot was easy enough for Alice to do alone. She even felt like she looked like she'd done it a million times.

"It's kind of cool," Theo said, standing in front of the blaze as it flickered its flames around the iron base.

"It really is," Alice agreed. "Okay, here you go." She handed Theo the bowl filled with sliced apples and peeled oranges. Then she used an iron rod to tip the cauldron forward, allowing just enough space for Theo to pour in the fruit. She followed up with the spices. Then they both slowly poured just enough water in to cover the mix.

Theo was thrilled. He seemed proud of his kitchen skills and had the goofy, confident grin to prove it. When he turned his look toward Alice, she had already been watching every move he was making. "I can't wait. But you said it takes a while; how long do we wait?"

"Is five hours too many?" Alice asked, wondering if maybe they should have done this over the weekend.

Theo thought about it, but it didn't take long to shuffle through his priorities. Staying up all night and being dog-tired the entire next day to be with the one woman who somehow made everything seem right? Or being alert the next day on the job?

The woman, for sure. Theo lifted his brows at the thought. He must have fallen hard because only a few weeks ago, he would have high-tailed it out of there. And now, here he was, imagining himself moving in.

"I'd wait all night if that's how long it took."

"In that case, movie and pie?" Alice suggested.

"This is quickly turning into the best night of my life. What kind of pie?"

Alice moved toward her kitchen and leaned on the counter near a pie rest. She lifted the top and asked, "How do you feel about apple blueberry?"

"Like it might be my new favorite."

"You pick the movie. I'll dish the pie."

Five hours later, Alice's apartment smelled of all the happy aromatic aromas of autumn. The scent of apples and cinnamon danced in the air as the fire fluttered out beneath it. An old black and white movie played on the television that had been discarded hours ago. Two empty dishes, with blueberry smears across them, sat on the ottoman. And Alice and Theo were nestled into the couch, each with a blanket tossed over them. Grumbles snored lightly on the floor just beneath them, and Alice and Theo both had a hand resting on top of him. Neither had slept so soundly since Theo had driven into town.

CHAPTER 27

"We slept together!" Alice squealed into the phone.

"What time is it?" Riley asked through a drowsy yawn.

Alice checked the clock on her wall while she held her apartment door open for Grumbles. "It's four," Alice said the time like it was completely normal for her to be having the conversation at four in the morning.

"Did you say you slept together? Like, *slept together,* slept together?" Finally, Riley was waking up enough to put the earlier pieces of the conversation together.

"Yes!" This time the enthusiastic response was a whisper. Alice didn't want to wake her neighbors, and she definitely didn't want to draw the unwanted attention of the love potion-drinkers. She was feeling too good this morning to deal with that type of a distraction – even though Theo *was* one of those people.

"How? What? When?"

Alice visualized Riley sitting up in bed.

"Wait, don't say anything. I'm coming in."

"I'll add an extra dose of ginseng to your latte." Alice heard the lip smack of Riley's kiss through the receiver and smiled.

By the time Riley walked in, Alice had two lattes made and a bowl of fresh pumpkin with whipped cream on the floor for Grumbles. Alice was sitting on the counter, savoring every sip – and every moment from the night before.

Riley said nothing, just walked to her latte, sipped, closed her eyes, sipped again, then sat next to Alice.

"Tell me *everything,*" Riley said when she was ready to give Alice her full attention. "But start with how you ended up *in bed* with him."

Alice furrowed her brows, questioning Riley's choice of words. Then it clicked. "Oh, we actually *slept* together, slept together. Not, you know…*slept together!*" Alice's eyes grew wide. "We fell asleep on the couch after huge pieces of Franny's apple blueberry pie and a movie. We tried to stay up until the cider was finished, but we didn't make it. The whole night was…perfect." Alice got lost in a daydream look. "I think he thought so, too."

Alice and Riley sipped their lattes.

"Oh!" Alice startled Riley, causing a drip of hot latte to bounce out of the mug when Riley fumbled with it. "And he had the cider this morning."

Riley shook off her hand. "And? What did he say?"

Alice shrugged. "That it was delicious. And it *is* delicious." Alice elbowed Riley playfully.

Riley couldn't help her laugh and the happy feeling she had for her best friend – for her family.

"What?" Alice asked, waiting for Riley to give her a *be careful* speech or ask the *are you sure you want to do this* question. And the truth was, Alice wasn't ready for that. And she didn't know what to do – or what she would do. But for now, she knew that she needed Theo – and that she couldn't explain why.

Riley smiled and shook her head softly. "Nothing." She shrugged back to Alice. "Nothing at all. It's…refreshing. Like fall is new and beautiful, that's what you seem like to me." Riley rolled her head back to hover over her latte, then sipped again. "Who am I to suggest you do anything different than you're doing right now when knowing what you're doing makes you so happy?"

Alice leaned on Riley's shoulder.

Love you. Alice sent the thought to Riley.

"You, too," Riley answered her out loud.

CHAPTER 28

Theo couldn't remember the last time he'd been up at four in the morning *after* a night of sleep. Getting up for work on a typical day wasn't too difficult for him, but he'd be lying if he said he considered himself a morning person.

But waking up next to Alice, feeling the warmth of her body as she lay draped over him on the couch, their hands touching as they hung over the edge and rested on Grumbles. Well, if he could have frozen that moment and re-lived it every day, he would have sold his soul to make it happen.

Their wake-up was admittedly a little awkward, realizing they'd fallen asleep like that. Nevertheless, Theo grinned at the memory of their unintended, intimate position. And watching Alice wipe the morning drool out of the side of her mouth, and being self-conscious about the way her hair looked, was worth every unfamiliar second.

But they'd bumbled past the insecure moment and had been able to transition to a morning that felt natural. He liked the way she'd gotten up and put a pot of water on the stove for some tea. And the way she'd slid her bare feet into fluffy slippers before crossing the cool floor.

When she'd asked him if he was ready, while she'd stood cradling her tea just below her chin, he hadn't the slightest idea what she'd been talking about. But then she motioned to the cauldron that had been simmering all night, and he remembered feeling excited.

Who in their right mind is excited for apple cider at four in the morning? Or for anything at that hour of the day, for that matter?

Even now, the thought was fascinating. In fact, it was just as impressive as the process.

They'd tipped the cauldron to empty the juicy mix back into a giant bowl. They'd mixed, mashed, and smashed everything together using wooden utensils he'd never seen before. Then, they'd strained all of that fragrant, cloudy, amber liquid into two clear glasses. And for a moment, he'd just stared at it.

There'd been so many thoughts flying around his head as he stared at that glass.

Should he be nervous? Was there something in the apple cider? How could there be anything in the cider? He'd helped make it! He made apple cider!

When Alice had lifted her glass to him, he had raised his in return. "Cheers!" they'd both said, clinking their glasses and taking the first sip together.

Now, three hours later, Theo dropped his head in a laugh remembering the entire scene. Laughing at the nerves he'd had. And, what was really the best apple cider he'd ever had. It was pretty darn close to the best *drink* he'd ever had.

After all of the to-do about the cider, the only conclusion he could come to was: *maybe the apple cider was just so good that it made people* feel *like they wanted to be in love.*

Ridiculous, he knew. But hey, it was darn good cider.

Theo laughed aloud then and pushed up from his bed. Being up at four allowed him the time to walk back to his own apartment, take a long, warm shower, and sit on his bed in a towel and watch the early morning news. That, too, was something he could get used to.

By four that afternoon, Theo was wondering how the day had taken such a turn. And, for the worse.

"Stop! All of you." Theo lifted his hands toward the room full of adults like he was playing *Red Light, Green Light* with a room full of toddlers. Then repeated, mostly so he could sound as defeated as he felt, he mumbled, "Just, *please* stop."

His eyes moved from one side of the conference table to the other, daring the next person to say something so he could effectively cut them off.

Theo pointed to his left. "Mrs. Hendricks. I don't care that you think Alice is *more delectable than Franny's pecan caramel rolls.*"

He moved a finger one person to the right, then waffled between the next two.

"Stephanie. Noah. For goodness sake. You two love *each other!* Not Alice. This is like a crummy episode of the latest dating show. Do not be those people!"

His eyes widened, sending a silent warning that reminded them it was their turn to stay quiet.

Theo rubbed a hand along his jaw, then motioned it toward Josh. "Buddy, you make beautiful bouquets – no question. But sending Alice twenty of them is not going to get you closer to her. It probably also isn't great for your bottom line. Last I heard, free flowers didn't pay the rent."

Theo saw the logic flicker quickly in and out of Josh's eyes a felt a glimmer of hope.

Progress!

Then, Theo continued down the row, looking at all of the latest to fall victim to Alice's love.

"Patrick, Cole, Blanche, Mr. Swenson–" Names started to escape him, so in a last ditch effort to keep his momentum, Theo said, "Beautiful townspeople of Lantern Lane."

Pacing back and forth in front of the table, Theo had to bite his lip to hold his straight face. It was mostly for effect but also to regain his composure because Beck almost had him cracking up when he turned and saw her covering her mouth at his scolding.

Finally, he stopped in the middle of the table, did a quarter turn, and looked at them once again.

"This insanity *has* to stop. If I get a call about any of you, or if I catch any of you in the act of defacing public property with drawings of hearts or pumpkins, pictures of coffee, your interpretation of Alice in flowers in the town square." Theo stared directly at Josh, who slunk down in his chair just a bit.

"If I see you bulk-buying canned whipping cream, caramel sauce, or canned pumpkin – Mrs. Hendricks – I will arrest you."

"Lastly, Noah, please take down the wall-sized poster of Alice from your *shared* bedroom with Stephanie. Stephanie, if I see you at Witches' Brew before four in the morning – I will arrest you."

"Finally, Mr. Swenson." Theo wasn't quite sure how to go about this one, but it had to be said. "Please do not talk about your bedroom prowess. Please do not talk about it at Franny's diner. At six o'clock in the morning." *With other men who also look to be as old as the crypt keeper.* Theo thought and grinned as Beck muffled laughter into her hand from behind him.

Theo made eye contact with each guilty party.

"I will arrest each and every one of you if you fail to control your *lover-type* urges as it relates to Alice Balfour. Do you understand?"

There was silence. *Beautiful silence,* Theo thought.

But there was always *one* who had to revolt.

"Deputy Parker?"

Theo tried his best to intimidate Patrick – one of the newest members of the Alice-lovers tribe, but the one who could cause the most trouble, seeing as he was Paige's current crush – with a fear-inducing stare before answering. "Yes, Patrick?"

Patrick smiled in only the way either a too-confident or too-stupid frat-boy could and asked, "Do these rules apply to you?"

Theo blinked. *Well, crap.*

As Theo tried to think through the best response, he held his stern gaze.

"As Theo hasn't displayed any disruptive behaviors," Lane said, walking out of his office to the rescue, "no, these rules do not apply to him."

Lane looked toward Blanche, who started to object. "Blanche, as I understand it, Alice was paramount in setting you and Tom up not two weeks ago. And you've enjoyed each other's company very much. What kind of an image would you be making of yourself if you jumped from one lover to the next? Lantern Lane is a *very* small town."

Blanche closed her mouth – no small miracle.

Lane nodded to Theo, who sent back a nod of appreciation.

"Okay," Theo said. "You can all be excused. Don't forget…I *will* arrest you." Then for good measure, Theo moved his two fingers from his eyes toward the crowd. It was petty, but he couldn't resist.

Before Stephanie made it all the way out the door, she turned and raised her hand.

At least she received the stop *message.*

"Yes, Stephanie?"

The rest of the crowd stopped with her to hear what she had to say.

Stephanie looked around. "Will you be having the same discussion with Alice? It seems to me, if she could make herself less appealing, this would be much easier."

The group erupted in nods and mumbles of agreement.

Probably not possible, Theo thought as he considered all of the things that made Alice *appealing.* But it did only seem fair.

Theo nodded. "Yes, I will bring Alice in and have a talk with her as well."

It was ridiculous, but it would give him an excuse to call Alice and see her, even though they'd just spent the whole night together.

It was a Sheriff's Office, but when the building emptied, the people of Lantern Lane headed home, and stars came out, it was a pretty cozy place to be. Theo had lit the fire, turned on some old big band tunes, dimmed the lights – or, left only the back lights on – it was downright romantic.

By the time Theo had gotten around to calling Alice to see if she'd *come in to answer some questions,* she had already gone home for the day and then headed to Willa's for another round of pumpkins. He didn't want to make her turn around, and when she offered to come in later, at seven, just the idea of seeing her had him agreeing. Besides, it was his night to be on duty anyway.

Theo checked his watch and gave the room one last once-over – like he would have if he'd been prepping his home for a dinner date in.

Pleased with himself, Theo gave himself a little pat on the back just as the knock on the front door came.

He watched Alice wave to him from the sidewalk and waited for the heart-flutter to pass before moving to the door to let her in.

"Hey," Theo said after flipping the lock and pulling the door open.

"Hey." Alice smiled and lifted her hands as if to say, *here I am.*

And there she was. Wild, bewitching beauty. Her untamed hair had been pulled back, but the rebel red curls around her face fought to be free. It was the only disheveled thing about her. The lines of her face, her pointy nose, the freckles that dotted her pale skin – all of her was perfection.

Alice lifted a jar, breaking Theo from his examination. "I thought you might want some literal fruits of your labor."

"Good thing you didn't show up with this a couple hours ago. You might have been ambushed." Theo used one hand to take the jar and the other to take Alice's hand to guide her inside.

Alice laughed a little too energetically.

"Yeah," she said. "It's almost as good as a good old-fashioned love potion."

What are you saying? Alice reprimanded herself for her carelessness and felt a fresh wave of the guilt that had been plaguing her all day.

It had been fifteen hours of *should she, or shouldn't she?*

Should she tell him everything? Or shouldn't she?

Of course, when she'd asked Grumbles, he never sided with whatever way she was leaning, so he wasn't any help at all. Willa, who was usually the voice of reason – said that she *shouldn't* tell Theo everything and that she should just let the curse play out – which seemed terrible. And Riley, who was suddenly on board with Alice's happiness, said she *should* tell Theo so he knew the truth and could potentially break the curse – or die, which seemed equally as terrible.

Then, as if all that curse crud wasn't enough, she'd gone and given him a love potion. So, really, she wasn't sure which version of Theo was actually Theo and which version was love-struck Theo. And there *was* a difference.

On top of that, she didn't need love-struck Theo making any love-blinded decisions that would get real Theo in trouble.

What a mess.

Alice tried to clear her mind before getting to the Sheriff's Office. And as Theo pulled moved into the building, it worked.

She'd never seen it like she was seeing it now. The lights were low, the fire was blazing, and soft music was playing in the background.

Alice grinned and turned.

"Mr. Parker – sorry, I mean Deputy Parker – did you bring me in for questioning, or did you bring me in for a date?"

Theo slid up to Alice and where she'd placed her things on Beck's desk. "I hoped it could be a little of both." Theo shrugged. "I figured dating is pretty close to a torturous line of questioning."

"I'm suddenly finding I want to know more about your dating history." Alice laughed at Theo's comment. "Is that how you feel our dates have gone?"

"Aside from feeling like I'm competing with the entire town in a game of who-loves-you-more? No, they've been great."

Alice smiled, wondering if Theo realized that he just said he was competing for her love. Because she didn't want him to take it back, she left it alone.

Instead, she asked, "Have you eaten?"

Theo stood tall and proud. "I haven't, but I did take the liberty of ordering pizza. Do you like pizza?" he added, panicking at the idea of Alice not liking pizza.

"What kind of a question is that? It's pizza."

Theo visibly relaxed. He should have known better. She's perfect, of course, she likes pizza.

Pointing to one of the chairs by the fire, Alice asked, "Can we sit?"

Suddenly, being off of his feet sounded like the best idea in the world. They'd been going strong since four that morning. "I'd like nothing more."

"Want to tell me about your day?" Alice asked.

"Yeah," Theo said, loving how normal the question sounded. "I'd love to."

They ate and talked until the flames from the fire had died, and there was only a soft glow from the crumbled embers. This, too, was something Theo could imagine doing with Alice over and over again. But he knew it wasn't just the moment. Something about *her* was different.

He could have enjoyed her company anywhere. Down by the harbor, on a park bench, or hand-in-hand as they walked down the street. All of it would have felt just like this moment.

Except, there was one nagging thought he couldn't push out of his head. Sure, while they talked and laughed, it slipped to the back. But as the quiet grew, it found its way to the surface once more.

"Do you know that when you think about something for too long, you get a little crease between your eyes?" Alice leaned forward and pressed a finger lightly on the small divot in between Theo's eyebrows. "Just here."

The spot where Alice gently placed her finger burned like fire. It didn't hurt, but the spot where she touched felt hot.

"Alice," Theo started. "I need to ask you a question."

"Anything." Alice meant it. The agony she'd felt all day of weighing the options slipped away.

She decided then and there: no more secrets. If he asked, she would answer. And over time, eventually, he'd know everything. Then she'd deal with the fallout from the curse as needed.

Alice took his hand, and Theo ignored the soft glow that resulted.

He looked into her eyes and asked, "Alice, was there something in the apple cider that would have caused people to fall in love with you?"

There, he'd done it.

Theo watched Alice accept the question and not take even a second before responding easily.

Alice smiled and said, "I didn't give anybody anything different than I gave you."

To Alice, that was the truth. But she had a question of her own. "Theo Parker, are you falling in love with me?"

Theo grinned and dropped his head. He should have known better. What could Alice – or anybody – put in a drink to make people fall in love? He should have known the question wasn't needed, but he had to ask. He had to do the job.

Then, there was Alice's question. Theo lifted his head and brought his spare hand to hold hers in both of his. "I don't think there's any other word for what I'm feeling for you."

Theo stood as he heard *Autumn Wind*, one of his favorite old songs, flow throughout the open spaces of the building and pulled Alice with him.

Theo took Alice's hand and placed one on his shoulder, and held the other. Then he gathered her in. They swayed in a dance so close, so intimate, Theo knew with all of his heart, he was hers. Time had no meaning. He could have known her for a single day, or ten thousand. His feelings would have been the same.

They seemed to be barely moving, but it felt like floating. Theo knew he would remember this exact moment for the rest of their lives.

Because it was the moment he knew that he was in love with Alice Balfour.

"Theo, I have to tell you something." Alice's voice sounded like a whisper.

He heard her, but he couldn't let the moment pass. Theo looked down and said nothing. To his mind, there was nothing more that needed to be said.

When their eyes met, he did the only thing he could think to do. He pressed his lips to hers and let the ecstasy and electricity consume them.

CHAPTER 29

"Are you coming or not?" Alice shouted behind her as she hoisted Grumbles into the back of her car. "For goodness sakes, Grumbles," Alice grunted as she lifted the dog's massive rear-end. "You're a magical being! You're opinionated, picky about food, you *know* you're in good shape. On top of that," Alice heaved the door shut and nearly fell to the ground, but it didn't stop her, "you *should* have the wisdom of a ninety-nine-year-old man."

Grumbles poked his head out of the window and looked dryly at Alice.

"And you *still* can't climb into a car yourself."

The whining moan was long and pathetic.

"You're lucky I love you." Alice pushed up from the side of the car and watched Riley take her sweet time. "Did you hear me?"

Riley sipped her latte and waved Alice off. "Since when are you in such a rush to get to the aunts' house?"

Alice opened the passenger side door, then closed it after Riley piled herself in. She stuck her head through the door and looked directly into Riley's eyes. "Since my soulmate kissed me last night and sent those little fireworks that spin in curlicues all over the room."

Riley lifted her eyebrows, intrigued. "Like, really? Or, just *felt* like fireworks."

"The literal kind. I tried to tell Theo everything, he kissed me, there was a small combustion, we were floating, and when it ended, our feet were back on the ground."

"And Theo didn't find any of that strange?" Riley couldn't believe what she was hearing.

Alice speed-walked around the car and slid into the driver's seat. She placed her hands on the steering wheel and paused.

After taking a breath, she looked at Riley and said, "Honestly, I know he feels it. But, I think in some absolutely insane way, he's justifying it because the feelings are so intense. Like his mind is saying, *Hey, it's cool, we're floating. But it's because we're in love. Go ahead, ignore it.*"

"Yup," Riley said, agreeing with Alice.

"What do you mean, *yup?* To which part?"

Riley took another sip of her coffee. "To the part where you said that he's absolutely insane."

"I never said *he* was!" Alice turned in surprise. "Do you think he's insane?"

Riley shrugged. "I guess you did love-potion him. It's not really his fault."

When Riley smiled, Alice squinted her eyes, hoping to appear dissatisfied with Riley's responses.

Alice pressed the start button and faced forward, ready to head to the outskirts of town.

"What?" Alice asked, rolling her eyes at the feeling of Riley's unspoken words.

"You know the aunts don't like it when you drive."

"Yeah, well, I'm not going to hop on my broomstick in broad daylight. Besides, brooms are supposed to be for sweeping up before a ritual. I should curse the witch who decided to plop their fat butt on one and take off."

"And?" Riley knew Alice too well, ignoring her rant.

"And I wanted to bring Grumbles."

Riley grinned. "And…"

This time Alice shot her an irritated look. "And I crashed into the outdoor altar, okay. I think I got some residual spell on me for the next couple of days. Who told you?"

"Willa." Riley's smug look only added to Alice's frustration.

"But I did want to bring Grumbles." Alice defended herself.

Alice and Riley hadn't been two steps out of her car when Peach, Parsnip, and Clementine rushed out.

"Alice, you *know* we wish you'd rather ride. It's much better to get into the practice of magic while on the way here. Especially if you'd like us to work on you."

"But," Peach bubbled happily, "we are delighted you didn't destroy our altar again."

Alice narrowed her eyes at Willa, who was standing in the doorway. *Traitor!* Alice shot the thought directly at Willa.

Sit on a broomstick! Willa shot the silent message back.

"Not funny!" Alice finally said aloud as she walked by Willa on the way in.

Willa leaned in and gave Alice a kiss on the cheek.

Twenty minutes later, Alice stared at her aunts from the middle of a witch's circle – it only took nineteen of those minutes for her to regret the decision to come.

"I've repeated the evening's events *twice* already."

Parsnip smiled as if she couldn't hear the irritation in Alice's voice and screeched, "I know, dear. But three is a much better number. Why don't you give it to us again?"

Alice let her head fall backward.

"I tried to tell Theo everything – that I was a witch, that I accidentally gave him and half the town a love potion, that he's my soulmate, and that he's most likely cursed, and there's a good chance that we won't end up together or worst-case scenario, that he'll die. *But* he stopped me. Instead, he kissed me like I was the only woman left in the universe. The room started spinning, we started floating, little sparks that looked like sparklers fizzled all over the room, and when he stopped, we were on the ground again. I might have whispered something like, *Holy hex!* before he started kissing me all over again."

Her aunts hung on every word.

"And you said it's Day Eight? Of the potion, I mean?" Clementine asked for clarification.

"Yes," Alice dragged out the response.

"Don't get snippy, dear. We're just trying to help." Parsnip was the best at scolding. It was like being spanked with a loofah.

Alice dropped her head to the floor just beyond her crossed legs.

"Well," Peach beamed, "we think it's just wonderful!"

"What do you mean, *wonderful?*" Alice couldn't believe what she just heard. "The man of my dreams might *die!*"

Peace waved a hand. "Oh, not that, dear. Your potion. It's a very good one. To have such a powerful hold after eight days - and on so many people – is quite impressive. Our little alchemist! Perhaps you didn't disown all of your studies as a child."

Alice turned her head toward Riley and Willa, who were getting way too much enjoyment out of this. "This can't be happening."

"Alice!" Parsnip reprimanded again.

Alice forced a smile. "Sorry. I mean, *why thank you for the lovely compliment.*"

"I think we need to go discuss the situation."

Without further explanation, Alice watched her aunts get up and leave the room.

"What's going to happen to him?" Alice wondered, letting the worry take her over.

Riley and Willa moved across the room and sat outside the circle, careful not to cross the threshold. Alice looked to both of them, and all they could do was lift their shoulders and let them fall.

That was the thing about witchcraft: a lot of times, you didn't have the answers. It's what made it so dangerous.

"You really love him, don't you?" Willa asked, wanting to know for herself.

Alice nodded. "Right away, it was this weird, forceful pull. I was so attracted to him, even though I'd never met him. It's like seeing a stranger and wanting to meet them so badly it hurts. They consume your mind. And you'd go back to the same place that you saw them every day if it meant you might see them again."

Alice grinned at the memories of the first days Theo had been in town.

"But then, one day, he just *saw* me. That first day he decided to make a move – the love potion day – everything changed. Suddenly we were on the same page. We were talking, sharing, and touching. Everything made sense."

Riley added, "Like he's your soulmate."

"Exactly."

"We think we have it!" Clementine's scratchy voice cheered on the way in as the aunts returned, each carrying an armful of miscellaneous items.

"Have what?" Alice asked, hoping for *something* that would help.

"We think you're experiencing one of two possible scenarios."

Alice waited with the patience of an owl, but honestly, she didn't have the time to be kept in suspense. "And?" she asked while eyeing the various jars, bobbles, apples, a pentagram, and a boline. Alice narrowed her eyes at the knife she saw last. *That can't be good.*

"Oh, right." Peach started talking as if she realized it was her turn.

Alice rolled her eyes.

"We think that either Theo Parker isn't your soulmate, but your love potion is *magnificent*. Or, he is your soulmate, your love potion isn't working on him, and he's falling very much in love with you. Of course, only until he meets an untimely *end.*"

Alice watched her aunts set up around the circle and focused on Peach, who was wielding the boline. Peach weaved and hummed with her sisters, building the suspense as the knife waved in her hand.

Alice's eyes grew wide as she prepared for the worst, ready to lose blood if it meant keeping Theo in her life – ideally alive. Peach brought the knife down quickly and stabbed the apple, while Alice let out a shocked scream. Peach looked up, questioning the outburst as she carefully carved out a slice and popped it into her mouth.

"What?" Peach asked. "These rituals are hard work. I like to have a little snack to keep me going."

Alice heaved a breath of relief and wondered if other people had families as strange as hers. Then she gathered her thoughts and said aloud, "Neither of the scenarios you outlined is good."

"Well, it's a curse, dear. Typically, they aren't of a good nature," Parsnip said, very matter of fact.

"I just don't understand," Alice admitted, not knowing what to do next. "I have so many questions."

"Well, just ask them." Clementine pulled one of her legs beneath her, then another.

Alice looked around the circle at her aunts. All seemed to finally be in place for what they were about to do. But they all waited patiently for Alice to start talking.

"Huh, okay. Um, I guess, the potion. When does it wear off?"

Peach started, "That depends on you. How well you made the potion, how strong your feelings are for the one it was intended for; a lot has to do with nature, the location of the moon, and your cycle."

"My *what?*" Alice choked on the question.

"Your…"

"Yeah! I know. I got it."

"But you just asked–"

"Never mind. I figured it out." Alice said, feeling embarrassed. She tried to rush to a new topic. "And you said it wouldn't work on my soulmate."

"Right." It was Clementine's turn. "Your powers and potions would be rendered useless toward your soulmate. Probably even somebody to whom you just loved deeply. That's the problem with love potions."

"That doesn't make sense," Alice admitted.

"Sure, it does," Clementine argued. "At its core, magic is brought upon by natural elements. To use magic on a soulmate or lover would be going against nature."

Alice didn't accept the answer. "But Aunt Clarice used a love potion on Uncle Norman."

Parsnip waved the statement away with a *pfft* and a disregarding flap of her hand. "Clarice doesn't love Norman, dear. She loves his money."

"Oh," Peach piped in. "And that really nice house he has in France."

Parsnip nodded. "Besides, Clarice is always having to find new ways to get him to drink the love potion she has stocked. It gets a little dicey as it starts to wear off. Do you know how hard it can be to get a man to take a drink from a woman he doesn't really like that much?"

Alice ignored the snickers from Willa and Riley and left her mouth hanging open. *After all this time,* she thought, *you think you know people.*

"So." The realization hit her. "Do you think my potion worked so well because Theo doesn't love me?"

Leave it to her to have a soulmate who was actively trying to avoid women. She could help any old schmuck fall in love, but not herself.

"Oh Alice, dear, I think it's the most likely scenario that he *does* love you and that he *is* your soulmate. It's all been very calculated."

"What makes you say that?" Alice wondered aloud, searching for answers.

"I think our Bridget–" All at once, the aunts dropped their heads and paused for their irritating, ritualistic moment of silence. "Well, she just thought it would be funny."

"She has an interesting sense of humor," Alice mumbled to her cousins. But there was a bright side. "But he could also just truly love me!"

"Right!" Peach grew excited with Alice – pure shared happiness. "And because his love is so strong and unwavering, he'll probably die."

Alice pinched the skin between her eyebrows. "Can you please, just, stop saying that?"

"Sure, dear. Would you prefer another term? Wither, dwindle, expire, perish?" Clementine asked.

"No, thanks. I'd like to avoid the idea that Theo might not be with us in the near future, all together."

Her three aunts thought about it, and all nodded, but only to go along with her wishes. None of them seemed overly invested in the idea of avoiding the inevitable.

Alice dropped her hands to her sides, so they lay limply on the floor next to her.

Here she was, in the middle of a witch's circle, finally in love with a man who literally gave her fireworks, and it would all have to come to an end. She didn't want it to end. She wanted the mornings, the afternoons, and the nights. She wanted picnics in pumpkin patches and movie nights with the scent of spiced apples dancing in the air.

"I can't let this happen." At first, Alice's words were a murmur. Then she repeated it, determined, "I can't let this happen!"

She looked around the circle at the five women staring at her. "Tell me what I can do. I'll do it."

Peach, Parsnip, and Clementine smiled, proud of their young witch. And Riley and Willa gave a hoot and a holler for the decision.

Through enthusiastic nodding, Parsnip said, "It's actually quite simple."

The excitement died down quicker than it took for Alice to flick her finger and put out a flame.

"What did you just say?" Alice asked, her face completely blank.

"The solution is simple." Parsnip said again. Then she looked to Clementine and Peach to be sure she'd said it right. They all nodded at one another.

"You're telling me, all this time, there's been a *simple* solution to the problem?" Alice tried to keep her voice calm. Her eyes were wide with a look that was teetering on the edge of losing it. When she glanced at Willa and Riley, she realized they were pinching their lips together – both knowing better than to say anything…or think anything.

"Why, yes." Clementine reached behind her to grab the gargantuan spellbook from behind her.

Alice watched as the book was set down with a heavy thud. It gave the ugly book from *Hocus Pocus* a run for its money. And she waited for the rest of what was sure to be a terrible explanation.

"We will perform a quick little cleanse. Then I think we'll try a quick spell to counter the curse."

"And then?" Alice couldn't get the answers quick enough.

"Then I think you should tell your man the truth. The sooner, the better." Peach bobbed her head up and down, agreeing with her instructions.

"That's it?" Alice asked.

"From your side." Clementine thumbed through the decayed pages of the spellbook one by one, carefully sliding a crooked finger down each one, reading as she went.

Exasperated, Alice wondered if she'd reach a point in the evening where she'd know all of the information before she left. At this rate, she'd leave looking as old as the decrepit spellbook.

"Can you *please* elaborate?" Alice dropped her face into her hands.

"Of course," Parsnip said between humming and prepping the space for the spells. "*Hmmm, hmmm, hmmm.*" Parsnip paused. "He's going to have to…*hmmm*…know the truth…*hmmm*…then choose to willingly love you despite…*hmmm*…you're a witch." Parsnip licked the salt off of her fingers, then resumed her humming. "*Hmmm.*"

Alice nodded, taking in the information.

"And if he doesn't, then..." Alice rolled her finger forward, not willing to say what she didn't want the aunts to say.

Rather than speak, to accommodate Alice's wishes, Peach took a chubby thumb and slid it across her throat while making a croaking noise.

"Right. Got it." Alice shook her head at how absolutely nuts her aunts were. "Thanks."

"Anything for you, dear. Are you ready?" Clementine asked.

"Just get' er over with." Alice closed her eyes and prepared for the worst five minutes of her life.

When a cloud billowed up around her, Alice closed her eyes. She waited for the crash of lightning or the burn of fire – but nothing happened.

Then, she felt it. It wasn't pain. It was worse. Unable to stop it, all of Alice's memories and thoughts of Theo came rushing out. They were reading her mind like they were reading a book. Listening to her conversations like they were listening to the radio. Every moment she spent with Theo flickered across her mind like a highlight reel.

Then, they reached her unspoken thoughts.

Holy hex, Alice thought. This was going to be embarrassing.

Alice braced herself. She was just going to have to let it happen. Every humiliating detail. Everything from wanting Theo to kiss her to imagining him naked.

Mortifying.

Without warning, the wall of cloud fell, sending a puff of fog throughout the room.

Alice took one look at the smirks on all of their faces and slapped a hand over her eyes.

"Blue boxers, huh?" Riley asked, grinning.

"Just…no." Alice stood, stepped out of the circle, and said, "Grumbles, let's go."

"Hey!" Riley shot up from her seated position. "You have to take me with you."

Alice ignored her and the reminder from Parsnip that followed. "Don't forget; the sooner, the better. Good luck, dear!"

CHAPTER 30

Theo wore a silly grin as he thought about Alice the entire way to the Sheriff's Office. As he walked, he waved to everybody standing in line at Witches' Brew, then across the street at Mr. and Mrs. Hendricks, who greeted him with a friendly, *Good morning!* Then returned to their own happy laughter while moving into Franny's diner.

When they disappeared, Theo stopped dead in his tracks.

Theo looked across the street, then crossed over and pressed a hand and his face on the diner window. He watched Mr. and Mrs. Hendricks scoot into their usual booth, order their usual coffee, and pick up the menu, talking away like it was any other ordinary day.

"Hey, Theo."

Theo jumped away from the glass, startled at the sound of Josh's voice.

"Josh, hey. How are you today?" Theo asked tentatively as he slowly inched closer to Josh's face, looking for…what? A sign that he was still in love with Alice?

Josh carefully took a step back, looking as if Theo was the one who was going a little wacky. "Ah," Josh stuttered a bit. "I'm pretty good. Nice weather, good business. Can't complain."

Theo watched Josh step in a wide circle around him, making sure to keep a wary eye as he navigated the curb.

He knew there was only one way to find the answer he was looking for. "Hey, Josh?"

"Yeah?" Josh backed away one more step.

"Have you seen Alice this morning?"

Josh thought about it, then shrugged. "Nope. My guess is she's working." Josh nodded back across the street at Witches' Brew.

"Right, thanks," Theo mumbled to himself.

Looking up, he started running down the brick sidewalk. When he reached the bottom of a small Main Street apartment, he bent over and rested his hands on his knees. Man, he needed to get in shape. Theo inhaled deeply and stood, putting his hands on his hips as he leaned back.

"Okay," he said on an exhale.

Theo swung the door open then climbed the stairs. The closer he got to the third floor, the more excited he got. Unfortunately, he forgot the early hour when he started rapping his hand on their apartment door.

"Noah? Stephanie? Are you home?" Theo waited.

Just as he started to knock again, he heard a click from the other side of the door. When it swung open, he saw a drowsy Stephanie staring at him with half of her hair matted to one side of her head and dried drool on the other.

"Uh, hi." Theo felt a little guilty intruding on their lives like this. And what was he even here to ask?

Well, now that you're here, say something, he thought.

"Sorry about the early hour. I was just following up. Um…" Theo scratched his head. "Do you have anything to tell me today? Just…about…anything?"

Stephanie let the silly grin play across her face. Then she lifted her left hand to push back the mop of hair from covering her face.

"Wow," she began. "Good news really does travel fast." Stephanie held her hand in place and turned it around. "Noah and I were engaged last night!"

"You're…engaged?" Of all the unhealthy-relationship things to do. They were *just* arguing about who loved Alice more… weren't they?

"Isn't it the best, craziest thing?" Stephanie beamed, looking brighter than the glare off of her shiny new diamond. "Noah said he'd been carrying it around for weeks. He wanted to do it sooner but felt like he'd been in such a fog lately. I just can't believe it finally happened!"

Theo blinked as he watched the young lady literally bounce up and down before his eyes. The *same* young lady who had just been in the Sheriff's Office for questioning.

Though, he had to admit, who was he to judge when it came to things that made sense in a relationship? For the better part of three weeks, he'd been imagining fireworks, floating, and other seriously insane cosmic-like events when he was around Alice. Heck, it had only been three weeks, and he knew Alice was undoubtedly the woman of his dreams. Coincidentally, she was also the subject of his actual dreams – but that he'd come to enjoy.

"Deputy Parker?" Stephanie asked, bringing Theo back to reality. "Was there something you needed?"

Theo stared, then grinned. "Stephanie, not a thing. Just coming by to congratulate you. Turns out, I have a little love situation of my own to deal with this morning."

Theo didn't wait for Stephanie to respond before he took off back down the stairs. He heard the newly engaged young woman's voice echo down the staircase as he skipped down.

"Good luck!"

Alice might have been a witch, but she could stress-clean like any other powerless human out there. Only *how* she performed the task was a little different.

I Put a Spell on You was blaring in the background, shouting the haunting tune through the open windows, out into the center of the small town's main street.

Alice had cloaked the window with a bit of fog so passersby couldn't get nosey a glance into her apartment – and they would try because that's precisely what small-town people did.

And on the inside, every scrub brush, duster, sweep, vacuum, and soap bottle was scrubbing, dusting, sucking, or suds-ing each and every square inch of the apartment.

The magic made her focus, and the chaos was a necessary distraction.

Grumbles, who was draped over his dog bed, decided to sleep right through it.

She'd given herself a day to loathe and curse Bridget – her famed, man-hating ancestor. Then, when she was finished with that, she took some time to think about and analyze what she needed to do. *That* was the stressful part.

Alice knew she needed to tell Theo the truth. She needed to tell him about the potion, the curse, and just so all of that would make sense, she needed to tell him she was a witch.

"And, oh, by the way," Alice said in a small, irritated mousy voice, "I'm just your everyday, run-of-the-mill witch. Totally normal. Totally believable."

Once the sarcastic rant was out, Alice felt heavy. Her shoulders slumped, and she dropped to the floor. With her knees beneath her, and her arms hanging at her side, Alice thought about Theo.

He was kind. He was funny. He cared about her. He was attracted to her. But, above all, he trusted her.

"After everything he'd gone through. He trusted you." Alice let the heavy words sink in.

There were only two scenarios she could visualize in her mind. Well, three, but she was ignoring that one for the moment.

The first, she would tell him that she was a witch, that she gave him a love potion to make him fall in love with her, and he would think she was crazy and leave.

Or the second, she would tell him that she was a witch, that she gave him a love potion, and he would be angry that she gave him a love potion…and he would think she was crazy and leave.

Or…there was the unspoken, life-ending third scenario.

Alice lurched backward and laid down so she could kick and flail like a toddler throwing a tantrum. When she finished, she was flat on her back, staring at the ceiling as her apartment cleaned itself.

Alice convulsed in one last spurt of tirade while she shouted, "I just want Theo to love me and not die!"

"Uh, am I going to die?"

In her outburst, Alice didn't hear the door open. When she heard Theo's voice, her head spun to the left. Then, when she saw his face, she shot up, and all of the cleaning supplies in her house fell to the ground.

"No!" Alice said, wanting to run to him. "No. I mean, I don't think so. About the death thing."

Alice was almost entirely sure he didn't hear a word she said. His mind was too busy trying to figure out what he'd just seen.

She watched Theo lift a confused finger to where the vacuum had been humming away in between the couch and the coffee table. Then he slowly moved it to the windowsill where the duster had fallen to the floor. Then to the broom that leaned against the counter after working hard at sweeping up the kitchen.

"Are you..." Theo's words appeared to die off with his confusion.

"Cleaning," Alice offered, hopefully.

Theo's dazed look moved from the broom to Alice.

"I'm not seeing things, am I?" Theo asked, slowly, as if he just realized that everything he thought he'd been imagining hadn't been his imagination at all.

Seeing as she still couldn't lie, Alice began to shake her head, then softly said, "No, you're not."

Theo nodded his understanding – or at least his comprehension of her response. "And all of this." He pointed around the apartment. "You were doing that?"

Alice took another tentative step forward. "Yes."

He nodded again and brought one arm across his body and the other up so his hand could cover his mouth.

Feeling panicked, Alice stepped forward once more and begged, "Please, let me explain."

"Maybe start with the part where you said I might die." This time, Theo's words held an edge.

Alice held out her hands. "Okay, okay. Just, um…" Alice looked around. "Do you want to come in?"

Theo stood just outside her door. He looked around, then back at Alice. "Not particularly."

"Sure," Alice agreed. "That makes sense. Ah, right." Alice clapped her hands together, and Theo jumped.

"Sorry. I won't – I mean – I would never hurt you."

"But I'm going to die."

"Right, ah, that's a curse."

"A curse?"

"Yes."

"Because?" Theo led her down the path of no return.

Alice took a deep breath. "Because I'm a witch. My great, great, great, great *something.*"

Jeez, she wished she'd listened better to the details.

Alice sighed and continued. "Well, she cursed the women in our family."

Alice paused, waiting for Theo to say something. Apparently, when you're told you've been dating a witch, not much comes to mind.

"We fall in love, it ends badly…you die," Alice mumbled the last part, staring at her feet, and squeezed her eyes closed before turning her head back to Theo so she wouldn't have to see the look on Theo's face.

When the room stayed quiet, Alice opened one eye and saw the empty space in the doorway.

Theo was gone.

THE PROBLEM WITH LOVE POTIONS

CHAPTER 31

For the next two days, it rained. The dreary, gray, heavy kind of rain that only fall can bring. The kind of rain that should have been enjoyed. The kind that makes you turn on the kettle and make yourself a nice cup of pumpkin chai and curl up beside the fire.

But for Alice, it wasn't that kind of rain. Not only was she the one that was *making* it rain, but she was also sulking and crying in the middle of a puffy blanket, with Grumbles at her feet.

Paige had agreed to tend to Witches' Brew while Alice moped.

All of Alice's cousins had been by to check on her – and to give her hourly reports on Theo's whereabouts. He'd left her apartment, but he hadn't left town. And, if there was a silver lining, it was that every report she'd gotten relayed that Theo was alive.

By the eve of the second night, more than a single knuckle knocked on her door.

"Go away!" Alice yelled from her imprinted spot on the couch. Even Grumbles joined in with a long pathetic groan.

"Either you open the door, or we'll open it for you."

Alice listened to Riley's response and frowned.

Witches. Alice thought. They think they can just use magic for everything.

Alice looked at the distance between her and the door. Much too far for her liking.

"Fine, then do it."

The locks on the inside of the door slowly slid into their upright positions and clicked.

Alice rolled her eyes.

"Don't be mad that you're not as good at opening locks as we are," Riley said, letting sympathy fill her eyes as the friendly sarcasm slid out of her mouth. She was the first to plop herself on one side of Alice and give her a hug.

The tears started falling, and the rain outside grew heavier with them. Alice's cousins looked outside, then back when Alice started talking. They didn't need to say anything; they'd all been there.

"I am *too* good at opening locks," Alice sobbed.

"Okay." Riley pinched her lips and looked at Willa and Beatrice, who were finding it hard to remain composed.

While Willa and Bea were giving Alice a hard time, Beck and Franny were already making themselves busy in the kitchen. Willa and Bea would be there for tough love. Beck and Franny would be there for comfort.

"You're right," she said, not bothering to mention they'd been caught red-handed when they were little, stealing extra candy from their neighbor's house. If Alice had been able to unlock the door, it would have saved them *hours* of nagging and training from the aunts. Because, of course, they weren't angry about the stealing; they'd been disappointed in the girls' faulty craft.

"Well?" Alice asked, through shaky breaths, knowing they all knew what she was asking.

Beck moved into the living room and sat on the other side of Alice with a tray of tea. "He's fine." Beck set the tray down and handed a cup to Alice, who just held it in her hands.

"Good." Alice let the warmth seep through her hands. It was comforting – the tea – but all of her cousins, too.

After another minute of rearranging themselves into her tiny living room, Alice looked around. "Why are you all here?"

"We can't check in on you?" Franny asked, trying too hard to smile casually.

Alice squinted at Franny, trying to read her mind, but it was too much effort. "No," Alice huffed. "At least, not all at the same time."

Willa led off. "We figured you didn't want to go back to the aunts' house."

"You figured right." Alice couldn't help but jump in.

"So, we thought we could bring everything to you."

Alice turned, wondering if she missed the *everything* Willa mentioned. "Care to elaborate?" She asked.

Bea jumped in. "We thought you'd never ask."

"You knew I'd ask."

Bea shrugged. "Just work with me, okay?"

"Anything for you."

"Thanks. Okay, here's what we know: Theo is still alive." Bea lifted one finger. "We know that the potion has effectively run its course." Bea lifted a second finger, then a third. "And, we know that you *still* can't use magic on Theo."

"I hope this gets better because I have to be honest, right now, all of that." Alice circled a finger in front of Bea. "Mostly, it just feels like salt on a wound."

"It gets better," Riley reassured with a pat of her hand on Alice's bunched-up legs.

"We think it means there's still time," Bea said.

"Time for what?"

"To break the curse." This time it was Beck who piped in.

"And how do we do that?" Alice asked the question aloud but knew that was the least of her problems.

Problem number one being, even if they broke the curse, Theo most likely would *still* never want to see her again.

"Well, we don't exactly know. But, that's why we went to the aunts' house and grabbed…*everything.*"

Alice leaned back so she could watch Willa and Franny move across the room, each grabbing one side of a small leather bag. Then they waddled back over and let it slam to the floor.

"*What* is in there?" Alice leaned over and tried to peek inside the small opening where the zipper hadn't quite closed all the way.

Franny shooed her away. "Back. Back, back. We've got a lot to unload."

Alice scooted forward so she could watch as they pulled spell books, old notebooks on hexes and curses, vials, knives, and wands out of the bag. Then, just because they could, and because they weren't completely insane a laptop.

Because Willa and Franny were the most dedicated to the craft, they were outvoted and assigned to the spellbooks. Riley, Bea, and Beck took the notes. And Alice took the laptop

– and the food. A good study night was nothing without the food.

As it turned out, they were all better at eating than finding answers. They'd made popcorn, had apples with caramel drizzle, decided on pizza for dinner, and because that wasn't enough – and because Alice was mopey – they had spiced pumpkin donuts with ice cream for dessert. They also had gotten distracted from time to time because after the talking, the eating, casually looking at the books and notes, and more talking, it only seemed right to watch *Hocus Pocus* – what with it being a witch gathering and all.

"This isn't working." Alice sat up from her lounging position on the couch. She looked around and saw that not a single one of them was working. They were all spread out, bodies were pillows, and legs were draped over couches and the coffee table.

When Riley snorted out a snore, Alice pulled the pillow from behind her and threw it at her face.

"I just need to–" Alice searched the floor for the right words.

Rather than waiting, Riley helped her out. "Buck up?"

Alice squinted tired eyes at her friend, pointed a finger, and relented. "Yes." Alice sighed. "Yes. That's exactly what I need to do." She leaned back against the arm of the couch. "How do I do that?"

"You talk to Theo," Beck said.

"What happens then?" Alice wanted to know everything, but she couldn't see anything.

"You both have to decide to love each other despite your differences."

"You mean despite me being a witch?" Alice questioned Beck's answer.

"Yes."

"That sounds ridiculous."

"Have you *really* never seen *Practical Magic?"* Bea asked, curious that Alice really wouldn't know these things.

"Nuh-uh, no way. Not you, too." Alice said, wiggling a finger at Beatrice.

"What?" Bea lifted her arms defensively. "It's basically," Bea waffled, tossing a couple explanations around in her head, "pretty close to accurate."

"*Pretty. Close. To. Accurate.* Every one of those words is like a hypocrite to the other. Not to mention you're talking about a *fictional* movie. You've all lost it."

"I think we're onto something." Franny jumped in.

"Maybe then, instead of comparing me to Sandra Bullock – which, thank you, by the way."

Bea smiled. "You're welcome."

"Just tell me what to do." Alice let her body go limp.

"Do you love him?" Willa asked.

"Obviously."

"Despite him walking away from you, avoiding you, and ignoring your calls?"

"Salt. Wound. But, yes." Alice lifted her head to look at Willa.

"Then tell him. Tell him everything. Pour your heart out. At least then, if all else fails, you'll know you've done your part." Beck finished for the group.

Alice let her cousin's monologue sink in. "That's very non-magical human of you."

Beck shrugged. "I'm a hopeless romantic."

"Then what?" Alice asked after a bit.

"Then, maybe he feels the same way."

"And if he doesn't?" Alice asked, mostly to prepare her heart because she wasn't ready for the response.

Riley reminded Alice. "You've elected not to talk about the part where he doesn't."

CHAPTER 32

It was now or never. And it *really* could end up being never.

Alice had waited until morning, taking the night after her cousins had left to gather her thoughts. But really, when it came right down to it, there wasn't much to say or plan for when you were getting ready to simply tell the truth.

"Are you coming?" Alice bent over to look under her kitchen table, where Grumbles had scooted himself when she'd dropped some of her apple popover onto the floor.

Grumbles looked up at Alice with his big, doughy dog eyes and started lifting himself off the floor. His groan sounded something like, *I can't let you do this alone.*

Alice grinned and scratched the top of Grumbles's head and said, "Thanks, buddy."

After grabbing her green plaid jacket and putting on her rain boots – thanks to her sob-fest the day before, the ground was still sopping wet – she marched out her apartment door with Grumbles falling in line.

"Wow," Alice said, fidgeting with her hands as they approached the Sheriff's Office, "this town is *really* small. Does it usually take less than a minute to get here from my apartment?"

Alice realized she was talking to Grumbles like he was a human who she fully expected to talk back to her.

Rather than stop and pull open the door, Alice slowed, then continued right on by when they reached the office. Then for the next ten minutes, she continued to pace the sidewalk.

It's not like she didn't *want* to go in. She knew what she was going to say, how she was going to say it, right down to the amount of time it would take to say it. What she was putting off was the *after*.

"Worst case scenario." Alice started and looked at Grumbles. Sometime after the fifth pace, he had stopped following her back and forth like a maniac and laid with his body leaning against the building so he could watch his owner get her steps in.

Alice held up one finger. "Death."

Alice held up two fingers. "Second, worst-case scenario: he decides he doesn't love me."

Alice stopped pacing and felt her body sag. Theo not loving her felt just as terrible. But, there was only one way to try and make sure neither of those two things happened.

Theo sat on the front edge of his desk and drank the coffee he'd made at work that morning like it was critical to his survival. He wasn't avoiding Witches' Brew, *exactly*. It was more like a hard stop so he could grasp the reality of his current situation: *he* wasn't insane – which was a good thing – but he had literally been floating, sparking, and creating lightning. Most recently, watching cleaning items float in the air. And all of *that* was insane.

He'd spent the better part of the weekend forcing his eyes to stare at football games, but he'd be lying if he didn't admit it was the first time in his life he couldn't remember a single play. Instead, his mind was consumed with Alice.

Theo took another drag of the breakfast roast he was counting on keeping him going and watched the object of his mind pass in front of him.

Seventeen. Theo took the mental note as he watched Alice walk back across the window until she was out of sight once more. And if the last seventeen paces were any indication of what was about to happen, she'd appear again in *five, four, three, two...*

Theo jumped, spilling his coffee, as the door swung open, slapping the wall behind it.

With Kleenexes being the only absorbent in sight, Theo grabbed them in rapid-fire motion and patted at the hot drink that splattered on his shirt and wrist.

When he finally looked up, feeling the burn on his skin, he saw a serious and rigid Alice holding her place in the doorway. Her breaths were calculated and steady, her posture was determined. Then, in complete contrast to the breathtaking woman, was Grumbles. The mammoth of a dog bumped her leg as he trotted by and went right up to Theo.

Without breaking eye contact with Alice, Theo rubbed Grumbles' head, then watched as the giant brown mop circled and rested on his work boots.

Theo watched Alice try hard to hold her gaze. He appreciated the effort. She probably wanted to stare down her dog for being a traitor. The thought did give Theo a bit of a boost, and it was enough to cause his lip to twitch a bit. But he remembered the situation he was in.

Floating cleaning supplies. Floating cleaning supplies. Floating cleaning supplies. Theo repeated the reminder to himself.

Oddly enough, he wasn't as worried about the whole *death* thing, because honestly, it was the most normal part of the entire thing. Eventually – hopefully, when he was an old toothpick of a man – he'd pass away. It was natural. The idea and concept of death wasn't crazy.

Theo realized there was so much he didn't know. And seeing Alice again, looking strong but kind of worried, he figured now was about the time he would find out.

He risked a glance at Beck, who was sitting at her desk across the room and watched her give Alice a tiny nod. Theo looked back to Alice in time for their eyes to lock once more.

Alice took another small step into the room and held her hands together. Just as she started to speak, Lane strutted out of his office and began talking before looking up.

"Okay, gang. We've got a good day ahead–" Lane stopped when he looked up from his papers to see Alice, Beck, and Theo blinking at his entrance. He opened his mouth to speak but closed it when he looked at Beck, and she covertly shook her head.

"I'm a witch!" Alice yelled, startling the crowd's attention back to her.

She had mentioned it the other night, but to be fair, she didn't know how many of the details Theo heard before hightailing it out of her apartment.

Theo returned his attention to Alice but noticed the wide eyes of Lane before he looked away. He'd had a couple days to digest the incomprehensible information, but it was a little comforting knowing Lane felt the shock of the news, too.

"I can make spells – moderately well," Alice figured if she was telling the truth, she should tell all of it. "I know how to move things with my mind, with my hands, or a wand. I can *usually* read people's minds or feel their feelings, but not with you." Alice gave a slight shake of her head and chanced another step forward.

When Theo didn't back up and didn't say anything, Alice kept talking. "I make potions…for a living."

This time, Theo adjusted his stance as he ingested the information. He couldn't help but clear his throat as he started to weave the missing pieces of the last couple of days together.

When Alice finished her examination of his reaction, she remained silent.

"And?" Theo said, partly wanting Alice to finish so he could get some answers, but also because he didn't like seeing Alice like this. The worry in her eyes was apparent.

"And," Alice looked away, putting her thoughts together. Then, finally, she blew out a breath. "Here goes…"

Alice adjusted her shoulders and moved her neck in a circle, then got it all out.

"I think you're my soulmate. The fireworks, sparks, dancing on air – all of it – might mean you're my soulmate. But there's a curse. A family curse. I'd love to explain it another time, but mostly I thought if I could get you to fall in love with me, the curse might not matter, that it might – I don't know – dissolve or something." Alice lifted her hands. "So, I made a love potion."

Theo brought a hand to his mouth.

"It was meant for you. But," Alice seemed to find a bright spot, "I decided not to give it to you. I thought it wasn't fair to you to do that. *But,* by accident, Paige mixed it with the apple cider and gave it to the Fall Festival crowd."

"Oh, my–" Theo couldn't believe what he was hearing.

"Yeah, exactly." Alice chanced a glance at Lane, who was frozen with his mouth gaping at the information. Her eyes drooped, feeling terrible about what she'd done and what she was putting them through. She hadn't even begun to think about the trouble she could be in.

"So, that's it!" Alice tried to seem excited that that was the extent of the bad portion of her information. "But," Alice said, hopefully, "there's also this: I love you."

Theo heard her last line, and he couldn't quite describe what was going on in his head: Disbelief, followed by a flood of relief, then followed by hurt, then again by hope.

"You don't have to say anything." Alice rushed on. "But you should know that this," Alice pointed to her heart, "is just the same as yours. When I see you, I get these little bats that flutter around in my stomach. My heart does this thing where it feels like it's skipping." Alice hoped what she was saying made sense. But most of all, "When I hear your voice, it's like home on a perfect fall day."

Alice visibly relaxed. She'd reached the end. So, she'd finished with, "I wouldn't trade any of the moments we've had together for anything. Waking up next to you was better than any feeling I've ever had. Kissing you was like a dream. And, if I had to give up everything if it meant you might love me, I would."

Beck's sniffle reminded Theo they weren't alone. He watched her wipe tears away with a proud smile. Then he looked down, trying to process.

What was he supposed to say to that? Theo's mind couldn't keep up with everything he'd just heard. Alice was talking like all of this stuff was completely normal. And *that* was not normal. Then, on top of everything else, was the paperwork. She had just added some significant information to the town's Alice-obsession case.

Without looking up, Theo said, "I didn't drink the apple cider."

Alice looked up, trying to stifle her emotions. "That' means you're my–

I think you should go."

"But." Alice started, but Theo stopped her.

"Please."

Grumbles whined at his feet, and it just about killed him. He bent down to rest on a knee and rubbed his hands over the big dog. Then he got up and walked into Lane's office and closed the door.

CHAPTER 33

As far as Theo knew, he was still alive. He didn't have any more information on the curse or the love potion, but he was still breathing, and everything in the town was still quiet.

And because he found he couldn't sleep at night, *and* because he was unable to ignore Alice completely, Theo had gotten into the habit of getting up early to take a morning walk.

It wasn't like he was spying on her. It was just coincidence that the route he took down by the harbor and back up through town *happened* to take him by Witches' Brew – which just happened to be right beneath Alice's apartment.

For two days, he'd made his own coffee at home, taken a walk, then sat on what he decided was his favorite bench.

Today, he watched the light from Alice's window flick on, sending a nice glow out into the dark morning.

Every once in a while, he'd see her walk by the window, pause, then turn back the other way. If her motions were the same as they were when he'd spent the night, he could imagine in vivid detail the way she moved to her teapot, lit the flame beneath it, then waited for the long howl that reminded him of a train sounding on a cool morning.

Theo took another sip of cold coffee and thought about her actions. They were so normal. As normal as his morning walks – though marginally less calculated.

Alice would finish her tea with her feet beneath her on the couch. She'd let the weather channel news change over at the four o'clock hour because it was too early for the local news, then she'd get up to dress. She'd wear something adorable – that would most likely drive him crazy – and decide what to do with her wild red curls. Whether she pulled them back or let them down, by the end of the day, they'd be frazzled around her narrow, *bewitching* face.

To admit that he'd fallen for her spell – whether intentional or not – was an understatement.

Then, she'd hop down the back stairs with Grumbles trailing behind and walk into Witches' Brew for a day filled with coffee and customers.

A normal day of work, Theo thought, *just like the rest of us.*

Theo threw back the last of the coffee and cringed at the bitter taste of the now cold brew. He tossed his empty cup into the iron trash can next to him, then pushed up and crossed the road.

There was no use heading back home; he'd only sit and think about heading into work. So, he unlocked the door to his new office – one that he realized he couldn't leave even if he tried – and moved inside.

Maybe he could use the three hours before his shift to figure out a not crazy way to fill out the paperwork on the recent vandalism.

Then, after a bit, he'd call across the street and place a breakfast order with Franny. He'd ask Franny how she wanted to proceed with the report – seeing as her window was the one that took the brunt of the pie-throwing and whipped cream tagging.

Already comfortable in his new routine, Theo threw his jacket and hat over his chair and moved to the fireplace. He tossed a couple logs on the grate, then used one of the long matches sitting in a jar on the mantel to light the starter.

By the time he walked to the kitchen, started the coffee, read the front page highlights of the newspaper, and poured his first *good* cup of coffee, the fire would be blazing, and he'd sit and get to work.

But, maybe this morning, he could afford a little extra time to himself.

Theo filled his cup a little more, tucked the newspaper under his arm, and walked out to sit in one of the lounge chairs in front of the fire. Theo took another sip, set it on the side table next to him, opened the paper to the first page, and within seconds he was sleeping.

"I hope that dark spot in the middle of the paper isn't your drool."

Theo kicked the table, rocking the coffee back and forth, as he swatted at the newspaper to get it off of his face where it had fallen. Theo shot out of his new napping chair, flattened his shirt and pants out of habit to appear put together, and saw Lane casually sipping a latte from Witches' Brew, with his eyebrows raised behind the cup.

"Did you sleep here?" Lane asked as he brought the drink away from his face.

"No, I've just been...up early." Theo shrugged, signaling its insignificance. It was true enough.

Lane leaned forward and rubbed his pointer finger on the side of his face. "You've got a little–"

Theo rubbed at the side of his mouth. When he pulled his hand away, he saw a black smudge, then kept wiping while he rolled his eyes. Then, he motioned his chin in the direction of Lane's latte. "I see you're not avoiding the local witch."

Lane lifted his shoulders. "Why would I? She makes a mean autumn latte. She's my long-time friend. Seems to me nothing really changed between the two of us. I just know a little more about her."

Theo pointedly placed his hands on his hips and looked down. When he looked up again, he asked, "So, you don't find anything out of the ordinary about Alice telling me – us – that she's a witch?"

Lane shrugged again. "I guess in the back of my mind I always thought there was a little more at play, but no. It's never – aside from recently – disrupted the town. I know Alice as a person, a friend, a business owner. There's nothing I think she could tell me at this point that would change my mind about how I feel toward her."

Lane moved his head from side to side in contemplation. "Unless you croaked. I heard that thrown around the other day. I'd probably care about that."

Theo rolled his eyes. "Glad to see you're taking this seriously."

"Hey, Alice is Alice. And I think you know that you are in love with Alice."

Theo stretched out his arms, hoping to get Lane to understand the predicament he was in. "She tried to love-potion me."

"But she didn't, right? And, when you didn't know that she tried, you loved her anyway."

It was a decent point, Theo had to admit. But still, he asked, "You honestly wouldn't care?"

Lane thought about it. "I think I'd be honored if somebody loved me enough to love-potion me."

Theo blinked. "And the witch thing?" He was beginning to feel defeated. "Nothin' there? Just totally okay with that?"

"Does it make her a different person?"

"Yes. It literally makes her extraordinarily different."

"I mean, at her core. You know who she is. You've been in her home. You've eaten with her. Gone on dates with her. She has a day job. Those are all normal, you-and-me, things."

Theo thought back to the date, the dinner, and the cauldron. *Son of a scarecrow.* "You don't think she knows how to levitate things, do you?"

Lane lifted a single eyebrow while enjoying another sip. "Probably," he said after swallowing.

Theo thought about it. "I think I really was electrocuted."

"Really? By what?" Lane asked, now curious.

Theo looked down, thinking back to the first time he and Alice touched. "Lightning." He gave a disbelieving laugh at the thought. "And the fireworks."

Theo looked up. "I had fireworks coming out of my…well, *everywhere.* Actual fireworks. Also…" Now he was feeling a little full of himself. "When I kiss Alice, I can fly."

"You can *fly?*" Lane needed the confirmation.

Theo noncommittally moved his arms. "Fine, I can float."

"Still pretty cool, though."

"What in the heck are we talking about here?" Theo turned to pace, then marched to square off with Lane. "This is insane."

Theo grabbed Lane's shoulders and shook him a bit to get his attention. "Do you realize the things we are *saying?* It's…not real."

Lane was quiet for a minute, letting Theo's logic sink in.

"Did you *like* having dinner with Alice?"

"Yes." Easy answer. Though, Theo didn't quite know where Lane was going with his leading questions.

"Did you enjoy spending time together, waking up together?"

"Yes." Theo tried to make it sound like he was hesitating, but the truth was, he did enjoy those things. In fact, he loved them.

"Do you love her?"

"That's not the same?"

"Isn't it?" Lane asked.

"No," Theo said, sounding unsure.

"How?"

Theo went to speak, but he couldn't. And not because he *couldn't* talk, but because there was nothing to say.

After a moment, Lane asked again, "Do you love her?" He enunciated every word.

Theo looked up with hope in his eyes for the first time since he saw Alice juggling every home tool, utensil, and cleaning device with only her mind.

"Yes," he said. "I do."

Theo wavered once and asked, just for one final bit of encouragement. "You'd fall in love with a witch?"

Lane thought about it, his eyes growing devious. "Think of all the things you could do in the bedr–"

"You know what, I'm going to stop you right there."

"Just sayin'."

The twinkle in Lane's eye was still there when Theo sprinted out the door.

CHAPTER 34

Alice was a witch of routine. Every morning, for as long as she could remember, she'd done the same thing – except for the past few because she decided it was perfectly acceptable to wallow in her own misery.

But after spilling her love-guts to Theo the day before, it had made her feel noticeably lighter.

So today, she woke early, had her tea, watched the weather channel that reminded her that she lived in the best place in the world during the fall season, and she had every intention of going to work.

Instead, when the latest hour of weather came to an end, she leaned forward and eyed the spellbook that had been sitting on her coffee table for the last couple of days. It was open to the page where Willa had left it when they had collectively given up their search for answers.

Before she knew it, Alice was five pages in and reading like a maniac. She used both hands to scroll through and flip the pages while her pen hovered over a notebook scrawling endless notes.

Now and then, she'd re-read a section, mumbling some of the words to herself. *"Curse holds true…Must prove worthy…"*

On the next line, her pen stilled, suspended over the paper.

Alice straightened, turned, and blinked at Grumbles, dumbfounded. He looked up from where he was resting his head on his paws, having noticed the change in her.

When Alice pointed to the book, Grumbles stretched, sticking his tail straight into the air, then walked over.

"Well, don't hurry on my account or anything," Alice joked, then massaged Grumbles' ears. Finally, she took a cleansing breath and said, "I think I have it."

Her finger found the lines of text, and she read them aloud.

"The entirety of one's being must be surrendered." Her finger forged on with her eyes with her voice trailing behind. *"For any curse to truly break, one must sacrifice thy natural self."*

Alice leaned back onto one of her throw pillows and exhaled. She looked at Grumbles, who rested his head on her knee.

"Well," she said, "I guess I didn't expect it to be a simple solution. But, if it means Theo gets to live, it's a risk I have to take."

It probably wasn't the most logical thing to do at the time, considering what she was about to do, but she pulled out her phone and made sure Paige was good with running the show at Witches' Brew for another day. The response she received from the chipper young woman was a shrill, happy scream when Alice told her it was because she needed to find Theo.

Then she closed her eyes, tried to imagine where Riley and the rest of her cousins were, and sent them a silent message.

I'm going to break the curse. I love you.

Then Alice closed off her mind, so none of them could try and convince her to change her mind.

Flowers. The answer is always flowers.

Theo tried to focus as he ran across the street to the flower shop, but his mind was racing. Maybe he would add a pumpkin for good measure. Anything to help his cause.

Theo threw open the door to the shop and stalled when he saw Mr. Hendricks standing at the counter, opposite Josh. He held his breath and prepared for the worst.

"Oh, hey there, Deputy Parker," a chipper, Mr. Hendricks, said when he turned and looked at Theo standing frozen just inside the doorway. "Beautiful day to get flowers for a beautiful woman. Isn't that right?"

Theo nodded tentatively. "Ah, yes, sir. Who might yours be for, Mr. Hendricks?"

Apparently, Theo's question was hilarious. Mr. Hendricks doubled over, coughing out a chain of laughter that sounded a little concerning, but Theo couldn't help but chuckle to himself – even if he was still concerned with who the flowers were for.

"I still get my Babs flowers every week. I don't think I've missed a single one."

Josh smiled proudly, agreeing with the old man. Theo didn't have the heart to tell either of them about the last two weeks. Who was he to kill a good flower-streak?

Besides, he was just happy the flowers were going to Barbara Hendricks and not Alice. And, it seemed Josh was still feeling good, too. But Theo would know for sure in a few minutes when he ordered a bouquet for Alice.

Mr. Hendricks cradled the flowers in his arm and wiped a lingering happy tear off his cheek with a handkerchief from his back pocket. He nodded to Theo on the way out and said, "It's a lucky man who has a good woman to buy flowers for, isn't it?"

Theo dropped his head and grinned. Then, he looked up and said, "Yes, sir. It sure is. Have a great day, Mr. Hendricks."

"What can I get for you today, Deputy Parker?"

Theo turned toward Josh and, with just a bit of uncertainty, and made his request. "Ah, I'm hoping to get a nice bouquet for Alice Balfour."

"Sure!" Josh beamed. "Makes a mean latte. You got your eye on her?"

Theo eyed Josh. It seemed he really was back to normal.

Thank goodness.

"I do. Hoping to tell her pretty quickly here that I'd like to keep my eye on her long term."

Josh looked pleased. "I've got just the thing for you!"

Theo didn't know flowers – he learned that the first time he was in Josh's flower shop – but from what he could tell with the maroon-tinged reds, creamy oranges, and golden yellows of the flowers, it was a nice arrangement. Alice would love it. Even if she wouldn't be particularly fond of him after the way he'd asked her to leave.

Reflecting back on it now, rejecting somebody after they proclaim their love for you was definitely not the way to treat a woman you loved. But, in his defense, she had just told him she was basically a supernatural being. And that she tried to drug him into loving her.

Man, what would he have felt if he'd actually *had* the apple cider?

Theo had already been over the moon for her. That kind of love was a scary thing to think about. But then again, she did tell him he was her soulmate. But then there was the curse.

And his response to all of that had been only to ask her to leave. What a terrible thing to do to somebody who was supposed to be your soul's partner, somebody *perfectly suited for you in every way* – yeah, he Googled it.

"Well?" Josh asked, interrupting his thoughts. "What do you think?"

Theo felt a mix of excitement and nerves, but he put on his best smile. "They're as perfect as they could be."

As Theo reached for his wallet, he looked up to see Josh hold up his hands. "Your money's no good here today. Just make a deal with me."

"Sure, what do you have in mind?" Theo asked.

"If it works out between you and Alice, just make sure you come in and get her flowers every week, so fifty years from now, you can tell the next young buck in town to do the same."

Theo grinned. "You got it." Then he thought: *If I live that long.*

Theo jumped up and down a few times to build up his courage and get his blood pumping a little bit.

He didn't know what was going to happen when he went over to Witches' Brew to do his version of a love confession, but he was going to go into it like those players he watched on Sunday night football.

Theo shook out his arms, careful not to damage the flowers, cracked his neck, then pulled open the door.

When he stepped out, he saw Alice walk out of the Sheriff's Office and look up and down the street.

He watched her for a moment, then called her name.

CHAPTER 35

Alice heard Theo yell her name. And when she looked up, there he was, standing on the opposite side of the street, holding flowers and a tiny pumpkin.

If there was ever a man for her, Theo was the one.

One look, one touch, is all it took. And if in a few moments the world as she knew it would stop, then that's how it had to be.

Alice watched as Theo started jogging to the middle of the road. She lingered for a second, then with a hopeful heart, she walked out to meet him.

For a moment, they stood just a foot apart, but neither of them said a word. Leaves swirled in a gust of wind around them, and they seemed to both know that from this moment on, nothing would be the same.

"I know how to break the curse," Alice said, not able to wait another moment.

"Just…" Theo started as he tried to hold up a finger while gripping the pumpkin.

Alice watched him bobble it, then swipe at it to make the final grab, but when he did, he ended up smacking it across the road into the ditch.

"Ahh," he sounded while slowly setting the flowers down next to him. "I'll just set these here." Theo finished his sentence by pointing to the ground.

Alice bit her lip and nodded, trying to hold in her laughter. After all, this was serious. And he just murdered a baby pumpkin.

"Right, uh, can I just go first?" Theo asked, only waiting for a nod before he plowed on. "Alice, I love you."

Wow, all in, he thought, as he heard the words that spewed out of his mouth.

Theo rubbed the back of his neck and gave an embarrassed half-laugh.

"I like having dinner with you. And I like watching movies with you. And picking out pumpkins with you. I really like how it feels to wake up next to you – even if it was an accident. I think you're beautiful. But not normal-beautiful, like, magnificent-beautiful. Even in the morning, when you have a little drool dried on the side of your face."

Alice shifted, remembering the morning he saw her a little disheveled.

"No," Theo said, stopping Alice's discomfort. "I don't *like* all of those things," he corrected. "I love them. And I want them…over and over again. With you."

Alice started to speak, figuring it was her turn, but when she opened her mouth, Theo freight-trained on.

"And, you're a witch. That's okay," Theo said, more for himself than for Alice. "It's more than okay. It's great. In fact, I love the idea of never having to do a chore again."

Theo wondered what that might have sounded like, so he tried to recover. "But I will! You know, do chores if you want me to." He finally looked at Alice. "I'm butchering this, aren't I?"

Alice laughed and realized there was never a time she had felt more loved.

"No." She shook her head. "You're doing perfectly."

Theo blew out a staggered breath. "Alice, I don't care if it kills me. I love you. *All* of you."

Theo grinned and shifted his head just a bit to the right. "And Grumbles. I love Grumbles, too."

The tears found Alice's eyes as the happy laughter bubbled out.

"That's really good," she said, her words heaving through the overjoyed sobs.

Then she held up her own finger as she tried to gather herself.

She used the back of her hands to wipe the tears off her face, smudging her makeup in the process.

Alice watched as Theo bit his lip while taking in her emotional appearance, and she shook her head. "It's only going to get worse."

Theo laughed and nodded, accepting her excuse for leaving the black smears down her cheeks.

Alice inhaled a snotty, extremely unattractive breath, then blew it out. She smiled at the love of her life – her soulmate – and said, "I found out how to break the curse."

"Alice, no!"

Theo and Alice both turned to see Riley running toward them.

Theo tilted his head, not understanding what was going on. Finally, he looked to Alice, who smiled at Riley, and lifted her hands in a small shrug, as if to say, *It's the only way.*

As Riley yelled once more, it hit Theo.

She found a way to break the curse. If he didn't die…then Alice…

As Theo's eyes grew wide with fear, Alice closed the gap between them, and she pressed her lips to his.

When their lips touched, a surge of energy exploded around them. Fireworks sparked, and the street cracked and shifted.

Riley fell to the ground with the quake, and a small tear escaped as she watched.

Alice had never felt anything so wonderful, so freeing. The way their lips hummed, the way her body warmed, the way her heart swelled.

She would have given everything up for this one moment.

When she pulled away, she smiled brightly and held Theo's handsome face in her hands. He was worth it.

Alice felt the lightness and the freedom from the curse and decided she would have done that a million times over again.

Alice's sappy moment was cut short as Theo gripped her face. "What did you do?" He asked, looking Alice over, then pulling her in, cradling her in his arms. "Why would you do that?"

Panic filled every inch of his newly freed body.

Alice would have answered, but he was holding her so tightly to his chest she couldn't get the muzzled words out. Then, she heard Riley's feet patter on the pavement to where they were standing.

When Alice was able to loosen Theo's hold on her just enough to lift her head up and look between Theo and Riley, Alice asked, "What is going on?"

Theo couldn't believe she was even asking that question. He looked to Riley for some support in telling Alice she was crazy for sacrificing herself like that. But, since Riley seemed speechless and like she was barely holding back a flood of tears, Theo asked, "Did you just give up your life for mine?"

"Of course not!" Alice laughed as if the notion was crazy. "I gave up my natural powers."

She repeated the text she had read that morning. "*For any curse to truly break, one must sacrifice thy natural self.* I let go of my powers because I don't care if my broom can't sweep my apartment by itself, or if I'm not able to listen to random people's thoughts, or if I'm able to be *moderately* good at unlocking doors without a key. I want a full, long life with you, Theo. I don't need these magical abilities for that. What we have, is magic enough."

Then Alice quickly said, "But I still would have done it if it meant giving up my life."

Riley let out a laughing cry of relief. "You're insane."

Alice laughed at her best friend, reached out a hand to touch her cheek, then turned back to Theo.

"No," she said. "I'm in love."

THANK YOU!

I'm so humbled that you've taken the time to read my book. I can't tell you how much of my heart goes into each and every word.

I WOULD BE SO GRATEFUL FOR YOUR HONEST REVIEW OF:
The Problem with Love Potions

Scan the QR code below to be taken to Amazon.
(Use your phone camera to hover over the image!)

ARE YOU READY FOR MORE?

Keep flipping pages for:

A BONUS EPILOGUE

TWO NEW SWEET HOLIDAY ROMANCE BOOKS

A SNEAK PEAK INTO THE TAKING CHANCES SERIES

BONUS EPILOGUE

Do you want more of Alice and Theo?

Scan the QR code below to subscribe to Katie's Newsletter and get the bonus epilogue sent straight to your email!
(Use your phone camera to hover over the image!)

Coming Soon!

A Borrowed Christmas Love Story

KATIE BACHAND

A BORROWED CHRISTMAS LOVE STORY

A Borrowed Christmas Love Story is a sweet, Hallmark-style holiday romance that thrusts two people into the unknown love stories of their grandparents. Perhaps both were too quick to judge their grandparents' decision to remarry so late in life. And perhaps the love story they learn about isn't unlike their own.

Scan below for the Amazon Sales Page
(Use your phone camera to hover over the image!)

Coming Soon!

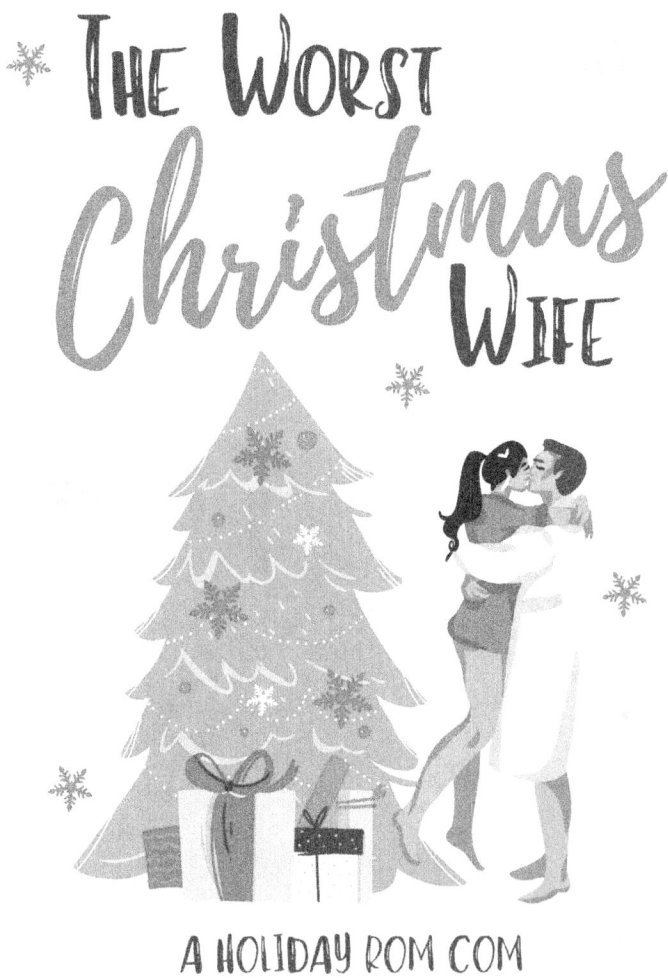

The Worst Christmas Wife

A Holiday Rom Com
Katie Bachand

THE WORST CHRISTMAS WIFE

The Worst Christmas Wife is a laugh-out-lough, holiday rom com about one (extremely handsome) grumpy boss that needs a wife, one over-qualified new assistant that needs a raise and a promotion, and two attracted-to-each-other people who hate that they need each other to make it happen.

Scan below for the Amazon Sales Page
(Use your phone camera to hover over the image!)

TAKE A LOOK AT TAKING CHANCES
A sweet (with a little heat) romantic comedy series.

TAKING CHANCES

Taking Chances is the hilarious four-book series about four friends who find themselves having to navigate unexpected romantic relationships. If you like strong and savvy heroines, hunky heroes, and snappy dialogue, then you'll adore this sweet and sexy series.

Scan below for the Amazon Sales Page
(Use your phone camera to hover over the image!)

BOOKS BY KATIE BACHAND

SERIES

Taking Chances Series:
Becoming Us (Prequel)
Conflict of Interest (#1)
In the Business of Love (#2)
A Business Affair (#3)
Betting on Us (#4)

STANDALONES

Romantic Comedy:
The Problem with Love Potions

Christmas Novels:
Postmark Christmas
Waiting on Christmas
A Borrowed Christmas Love Story
The Worst Christmas Wife

ABOUT THE AUTHOR

KATIE BACHAND is the author of contemporary romance, sweet romantic comedy, and wholesome holiday romance novels.

KATIE lives with her husband, sons, and golden retriever in beautiful Minneapolis, Minnesota. She hopes in her novels, and in life, you find great friendships, great love, and great appreciation for our wonderful world and the people in it.

Visit Katie on her website at
https://www.katiebachandauthor.com

Or, find Katie on any of your favorite social media outlets by following the link below, or searching **KATIE BACHAND** on Facebook and Instagram.

https://www.instagram.com/katiebachandauthor
https://www.facebook.com/katiebachandauthor

Printed in Great Britain
by Amazon